BIG BOOK

OF

KNOWLEDGE

— BLOOMSBURY EDUCATION

Bloomsbury Publishing Plc
50 Bedford Square, London, WC1B 3DP, UK
Bloomsbury Publishing Ireland Limited
29 Earlsfort Terrace, Dublin 2, D02 AY28, Ireland

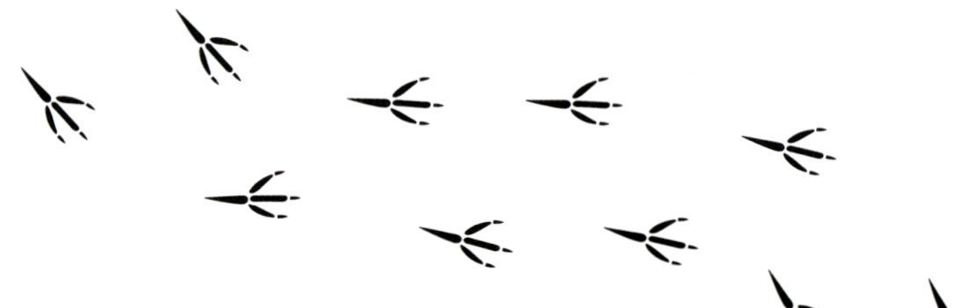

BIG BOOK OF EVEN MORE KNOWLEDGE

BLOOMSBURY EDUCATION
LONDON OXFORD NEW YORK NEW DELHI SYDNEY

CONTENTS

AMAZING

ANIMALS

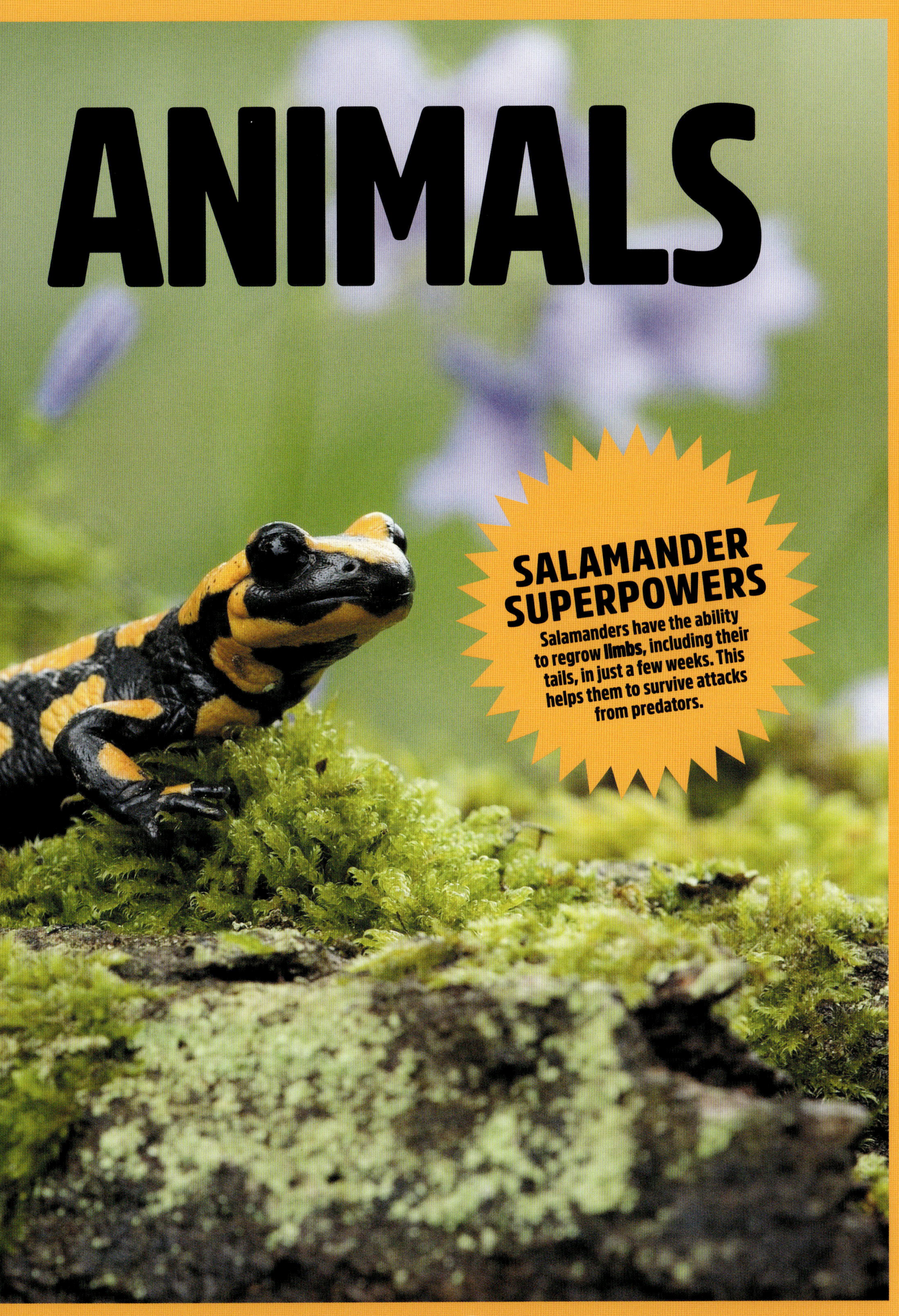

SALAMANDER SUPERPOWERS
Salamanders have the ability to regrow limbs, including their tails, in just a few weeks. This helps them to survive attacks from predators.

DARING DASHES

These adventurous animals all escaped into the unknown – but returned happily home afterwards.

Cheeky parrot's wild weekend

A pet parrot that flew off for a wild weekend in Glasgow, Scotland, was found at a local hospital and reunited with his owner.

Eight-year-old Jobby had taken trips to the park with his owner, Apsi Witana, but had "never flown away before," she said. People stuck up posters and put appeals on social media.

The afternoon after he went missing, a nurse phoned to report that Jobby was "eating crisps and playing around" in her hospital. Witana said Jobby seemed "in good spirits".

Runaway kangaroo hits police officer

After spending four days on the run in Oshawa, Canada, a kangaroo hit a police officer in the face.

The animal had escaped while being transported to her new home: a zoo in Quebec, Canada. She wasn't arrested after the police finally caught her, though: she was taken to nearby Oshawa Zoo to be checked over.

Budge Lightyear's adventures in space

The **RSPCA** was called to rescue an escaped budgie from the car park at the National Space Centre in Leicester, UK.

The wannabe space voyager was a brightly coloured budgie named Budge Lightyear, after the *Toy Story* character, Buzz Lightyear. He was moved to a nearby animal centre while the charity looked for his owner.

The RSPCA asked anyone who might know Budge, or who his owner is, to come forward.

While it's not known if Budge was reunited with his family, the RSPCA staff made sure he was well cared for, with plenty of food, toys, and a comfortable cage that was much safer than the Space Centre's car park.

Budge Lightyear to star command ...

GREAT ADVENTURES

Meet even more bold beasts who broke free.

Horsing around at the station

Travellers waiting for their train in Sydney, Australia, were surprised to see a horse join them on the platform.

The racehorse, which had escaped from its home nearby, walked down the platform and then patiently waited behind the yellow line. It didn't manage to board the train, though: it was taken back by its owner before it could continue its grand adventure.

I never get to ride anything!

Escape-artist lynx set free

In Saxony, Germany, a rebellious Carpathian lynx has now been set free.

The animal, Chapo, was part of a **breeding programme** to help boost the population of his species, but he kept trying to jump over the fence.

Experts eventually decided it would be best to set the wildcat free. He was fitted with a collar that could track his location before being released into a forest.

Real OR rubbish?

Santa's reindeer on the loose

Police officers were called to a Christmas crime scene in Suffolk, UK, after reports that a couple of Santa's reindeer had escaped. Police closed a busy road to try to catch them – but with no luck.

Order was eventually restored after a few hours, when the rebellious reindeer left the scene on their own. They seemed to know they were needed back at Santa's grotto.

Is this real or a festive fib?*

***Real!** The reindeer were part of a Christmas attraction built nearby, and managed to make their own way back.

FEEL THE BEAT

These animals really have rhythm.

Lemurs reveal our rhythmic roots

Scientists believe that lemurs' calls could reveal why we **evolved** to produce music with rhythmic sounds.

The honk-like calls of indri lemurs follow a steady beat that is similar to the one in human-made music. They include a higher number of vocal rhythms than songbirds and other singing animals.

Researchers saw that the indris sang for several reasons, including to greet each other, to show they were lost or to alert others to danger. They also had loud singing battles, seemingly for fun. Scientists say that singing helps the animals bond.

Can orangutans beatbox?

Orangutans can produce two sounds at the same time, similar to humans who beatbox, making noises with their voices that are similar to instruments and sound effects.

Scientists have found male orangutans in Borneo producing noises called "chomps" at the same time as "grumbles" before fights. Females in Indonesia made "kiss squeak" sounds at the same time as "rolling calls" as alerts.

Musical birds design unique drumsticks

Male palm cockatoos have a special way of attracting mates: they carve unique drumsticks to beat rhythms on trees.

Experts found that fathers teach their stick-crafting skills to their sons, but each cockatoo's designs are different. Some pick sticks that are short and fat, while others use long, skinny ones. Some even prefer seed pods. They **whittle** them down into personalised shapes using their powerful beaks.

Professor Robert Heinsohn said the process "is like watching a master wood sculptor at work".

CREATURES COME DANCING

Humans aren't the only living things on Earth to have mastered complex choreography.

A bird's favourite song

When a cockatiel was found at a church in Pennsylvania, US, one family believed it was their pet, Lucky, who had gone missing three years earlier.

To prove it, they told rescuers that Lucky had learned to dance to a certain song. They whistled the theme song of *The Andy Griffith Show*, a 1960s TV series.

"The bird started dancing," said an animal rescue official, "so we knew."

Fancy finwork

Mudskipper fish dance to attract mates. They twirl their tails, arch their bodies and leap into the air. They can do this from land or water because they are **amphibious**.

The hungry frogs that tap-dance

Scientists may have discovered the reason poison dart frogs do a kind of tap-dance using their toes – and it's more to do with dinner than dancing.

Researchers found that the frogs tapped their toes around eight times more quickly when flies were nearby, changing the rhythm depending on the type of surface they were on.

The scientists think this could be the frogs' way of getting flies moving, making them easier to spot and gobble up.

Beautiful ballets

Great crested grebes conduct a kind of water ballet. Couples shake their heads and run their beaks through their back feathers. Next, they dive underwater and collect weeds before approaching each other. It's thought that this strengthens their bonds.

HEALTHCARE HEROES

Some clever creatures can help improve human health.

Horses help patients

At San Giovanni Battista Hospital in Rome, Italy, therapy horses are supporting patients who are learning how to walk again.

The patients have either been unwell or in accidents that affected their movement. The horses have handles on their saddles that people can hold onto while walking to help improve their muscle strength and balance.

Patients also build bonds with the horses, which helps them to relax.

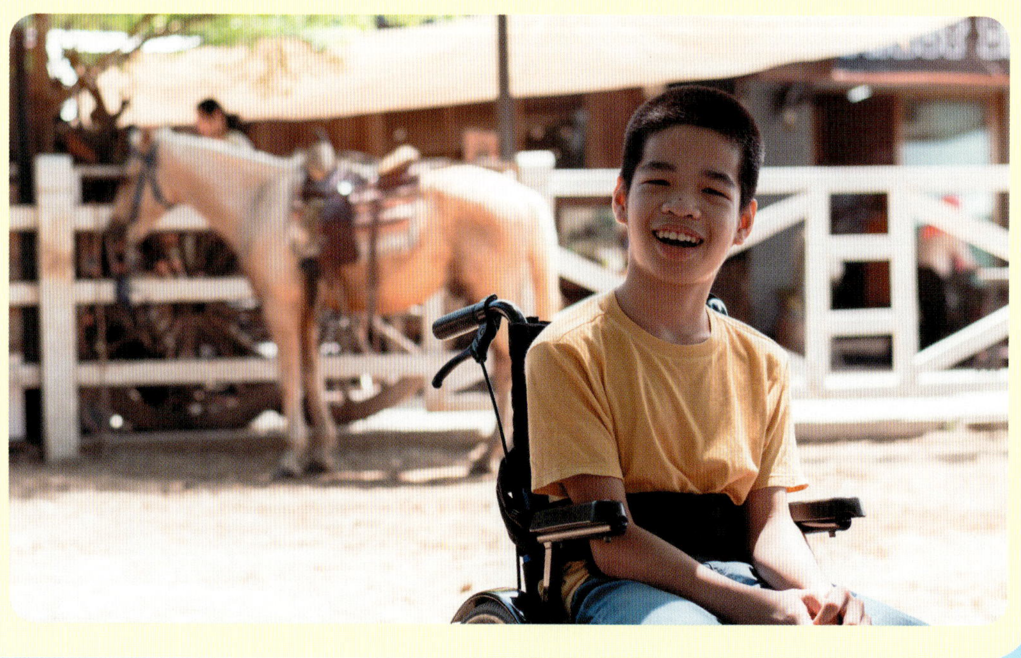

How animals help

Animals can be registered to help people in different ways:

- Service animals, like dogs that help blind people, give practical help during day-to-day life. They can lead someone on safe paths or do simple tasks like fetching or carrying.
- Therapy animals, like the ones at San Giovanni Battista Hospital, are used to improve patients' health both physically and emotionally.
- Emotional support animals keep people company to reduce problems like **anxiety**.

Whether helping with daily tasks, supporting recovery, or providing comfort, these animals make a real difference in people's lives every day.

Real OR rubbish?

The dog-tist will see you now

Dental worker April Kline's dog, Ollie, is now her colleague. During a special training course, he learned to recognise the scents of mouth diseases and alert the dentist if he detects one. This saves time and helps ensure no **diagnosis** is missed.

Is this the honest-to-dog truth, or does it not make scents?*

*Rubbish! Ollie helps out at the dental office, but only with greetings and emotional support. If requested, he'll snuggle on a nervous patient's lap during their appointment. Dentist Jennifer Herbert said, "He brightens everyone's day."

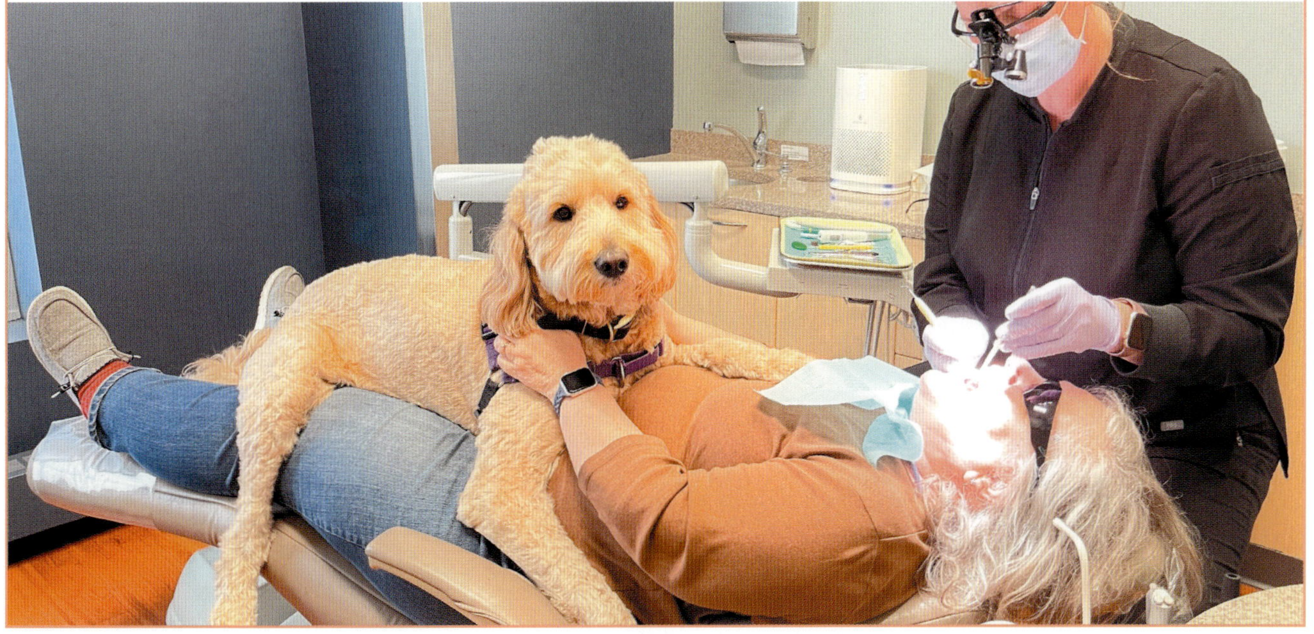

NATURAL
REMEDIES

Some amazing creatures use nature to cure themselves and other animals.

Ape uses a plant "plaster"

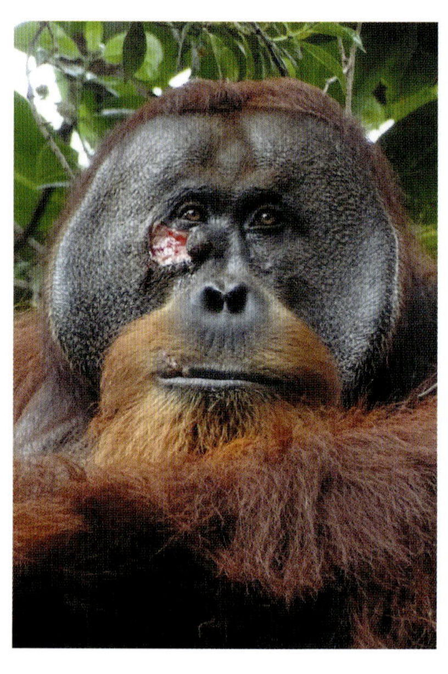

Researchers have seen an ape in Asia heal himself with plants. When he was injured, an Indonesian orangutan, named Rakus, sought out a plant called akar kuning. He chewed its leaves and applied them to his wound.

Akar kuning is known to relieve pain and fight infections, and is used by local people. After five days, Rakus's wound had healed.

Rakus before and after his treatment

Ants use natural medicine to save lives

Scientists have found that Matabele ants can heal injured members of their **colony** using medicine their own bodies produce.

When they attack termite nests to find food, these ants may get a kind of infection that's powerful enough to kill humans, let alone ants. However, Matabele ants produce an **antibiotic** in their saliva. Ants in a colony can recognise the infection, and lick each other's wounds.

Using natural antibiotics to treat wounds is extremely rare behaviour in the animal world, making these ants quite remarkable.

The chimpanzee doctors

Research has shown that chimps are using medicinal plants to treat themselves.

During a four-year project, scientists monitored the behaviour and health of 51 chimpanzees in the Budongo rainforest in Uganda. They noticed purposeful behaviour: for example, chimps found and ate a type of fern called *Christella parasitica* only when they were injured.

Scientists studied this plant and others they saw unwell chimps eating. They found that 88% of the plants helped stop infections and 33% reduced swelling. They healed wounds in just a few days.

It is very dangerous to try using plants as medicine unless you are an expert. However, the team thinks the plants in Budongo used by chimps could help to create new medicines for humans.

TERRIFIC TAILS

Animals can use their tails in many ways, including to communicate. Can you imagine life with a tail?

The many uses of tails

Tails help fish swim and birds fly, while lemurs' tails help with balance.

Elephants, horses and bison use their tails to swat away insects, and stingrays and rattlesnakes use theirs for **self-defence**.

Foxes' bushy tails are good for keeping warm.

Hippos spin their tails to scatter poo, marking their **territory**.

What can dogs' wags mean?

Tail-wagging may be more complicated than people believe. A study suggests that dogs' tails wag more to the right when the pups are happy, and more to the left when something makes them nervous. When its tail wags low to the ground, the pup may be trying to please or calm someone.

Dogs also seem to understand what other canine tail-wagging means. For example, when they see other dogs' tails wagging to the left, they show signs of stress. This suggests they've understood that there's a reason to be nervous.

Scientists say further research should be done. "We still don't know exactly which parts of the dog's brain control which features of the tail-wagging," said researcher Andrea Ravignani.

Finding a tail-wind

Sugar gliders stretch out the skin between their legs to glide up to 100 metres between trees. They use their tails to steer them in different directions through the air.

PAMPERED PETS

It's no surprise that people care for their pets – but some furry friends live in the lap of luxury.

Ice cream just for canines

In London, UK, dog groomer Emmie Stevens designed an ice-cream van exclusively for dogs. "Poochies Pupsicles" quickly became a hit with her canine customers.

Emmie's pooch-friendly menu included a "Doggy Mr Whippy" with gravy bone and doggy sprinkles and frozen "Pupsicle bites", which came in six flavours including banana, mango and peanut butter.

FUN FACT

In 2023, it was estimated that around a third of the world's households kept dogs, and over a quarter kept cats.

Cats rule at president's palace

Cats that hung out in the gardens of the National Palace, Mexico City, were given the legal right to stay there in 2024.

Wild cats began visiting the grounds 50 years ago, and regularly popped into presidential meetings. Thanks to former Mexican president Andrés Manuel López Obrador, the cats have been declared "living fixed assets", meaning the government has to feed and care for them for the rest of their lives.

Museum creates exhibition for dogs

The Museo Tamayo in Mexico City prepared special art **exhibits** specifically for dogs.

The works on display at the #ArteyPerros ("Art and dogs") exhibition celebrated bonds between people and their furry companions. It was intended to create a unique emotional experience for both human and canine visitors.

"The affectionate relationship that exists between an owner and their dog is always there," a museum **curator** said.

COSSETED CREATURES

Cats and dogs may be the most popular pets, but people pamper all sorts of other animals in their homes, farms and zoos.

A mouse in shining armour

Canadian artist Jeff de Boer became the world's first – and only – creator of mouse and cat armour, making more than 500 pieces.

His fittings have included a **gladiator** suit for a mouse and **chain mail** for a cat. The outfits are not meant to be worn by animals in reality, though. Instead, de Boer wants to spark people's imaginations.

"Each person brings their own story to my work," he said.

Cows' udderly relaxing retreat

The cows at LeeAnna Thomas's farm in Texas were treated to a life of luxury with regular spa days.

Thomas didn't just bathe the animals – she also moisturised their hooves and noses, gave them massages and treated them to face masks. She looked after the calves who needed extra support, too, giving them the pampering she felt they deserved.

"I always get asked how my cows are so gentle," Thomas wrote on social media. "It's because this is the loving and gentleness they receive."

The penguin that pattered in style

The St Louis Zoo in Missouri, US, certainly took care of one feathery friend. When a rockhopper penguin called Enrique got arthritis in his feet, keepers had shoes specially made.

The cushioned rubber boots helped the problem. They made walking easier for Enrique, meaning he could keep in step with his penguin pals.

NAP TIME!

Naps can perk us up and keep us going – and they do that for animals, too.

ZZZZZ
ZZZZZZ

Power-naps for penguin parents

Chinstrap penguins are the ultimate power-nappers. While nesting, the birds nod off for an average of four seconds at a time.

The birds may not sleep for long because they live in noisy, crowded colonies or because they have to watch out for **predators** approaching their eggs and young chicks.

All these mini-snoozes add up: with thousands of "microsleeps", the penguins can still manage nearly 11 hours of sleep a day.

HUSH!
Chinstrap penguins are also known as stonebreaker penguins as their cries are so shrill, they are said to be able to break rocks.

An award-winning napper

Polar bears are big nappers, especially just after eating. Snoozing helps them to save energy to keep warm in the icy Arctic. Polar bears love to nap.

The award-winning image shows how polar bears take every opportunity to nap – even when their homes are shrinking because of climate change.

A picture of a napping polar bear won a prize in the Wildlife Photographer of the Year awards in 2023.

Reindeer can eat while they sleep

For reindeer in the Arctic, food can be **scarce** in winter. During the warmer months, they must eat as much as they possibly can. All that chewing seems to leave very little time for sleep.

Researchers investigated by using devices that monitored reindeers' brainwave patterns. During chewing, these were similar to patterns during light sleep. The animals sat or stood quietly and were less likely to react. When the reindeer had finished chewing, their brain activity showed they felt rested. After eating, they also needed less regular sleep.

Researchers say their snoozy chewing "makes sure that their brain gets enough rest."

FROM THE BRINK OF EXTINCTION

Animal conservation is vital for saving animals from extinction. These four success stories prove it is possible.

Antelope species saved

A type of antelope, the scimitar-horned oryx, is no longer extinct in the wild. The oryx used to be widespread across north Africa but was hunted for its horns and meat. It was declared extinct in the wild in 2000 – but thanks to a breeding programme in Ouadi Rimé, Chad, 510 oryx have now been born in the wild.

Zoo helps out rare hippos

After 10 years of effort by animal carers, an **endangered** pygmy hippopotamus was born at Attica Zoological Park in Athens, Greece. There are only between 2,000 and 2,500 pygmy hippos left in the wild, and breeding them is difficult because there aren't many males in conservation sites.

Mini gecko numbers grow

Conservationists helped save a tiny lizard in St Vincent and the Grenadines. Union Island geckos were seriously endangered after people started illegally trading them. To protect the geckos, conservationists expanded protected areas and involved local people in patrolling them.

Thanks to these efforts, from about 2018 to 2022, the number of geckos almost doubled.

Bandicoots bred

Eastern barred bandicoots, which were declared extinct in the wild in 2013, have been successfully bred by Australian zookeepers. They are now being gradually released back into the wild, with trained dogs helping to protect them from foxes in a nature reserve.

ANCIENT ANIMALS

A scientist with some of the bones

Earth's heaviest animal

While the blue whale held the title of Earth's heaviest creature, recent discoveries have shifted that view. Fossilized remains, roughly 39 million years old, point to an ancient marine animal that dwarfed even the largest blue whales. This prehistoric giant, *Perucetus colossus*, could have weighed two to three times more than the blue whale, potentially reaching a staggering 340 tonnes. Interestingly, though its size is clear, scientists are still puzzled about its diet, as a skull has yet to be found. However, these ancient bones reveal that enormous sea creatures existed far earlier than we once thought.

Frozen jellies

Experts have discovered **fossils** of the earliest known jellyfish. They found the remains in 505-million-year-old Canadian rocks, meaning the jellyfish existed before dinosaurs. The fossils are so perfectly preserved that individual **tentacles** can be seen.

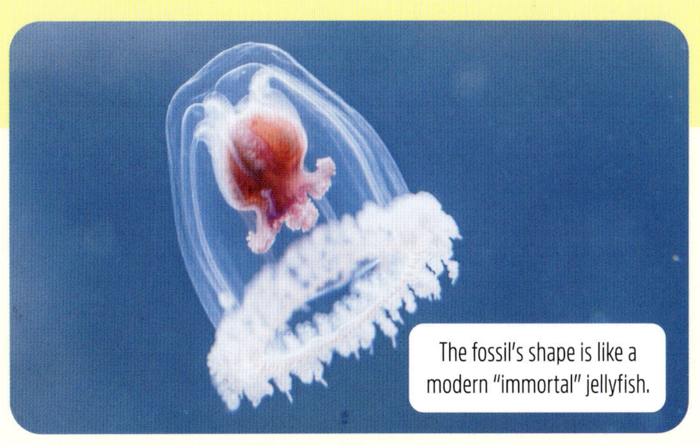
The fossil's shape is like a modern "immortal" jellyfish.

The *Gorgosaurus libratus* fossil

A dinosaur's full stomach

Scientists studying the 75-million-year-old fossil of a dinosaur were in for a surprise – the creature died with a full stomach.

The remains of the *Gorgosaurus libratus*, a slightly smaller version of a *Tyrannosaurus rex*, included partially **digested** legs of two small, birdlike dinosaurs about the size of turkeys. The discovery will help scientists to understand dinosaurs' behaviour, development and diet.

FUN FACT
It is estimated that a total of 1.7 billion *Tyrannosaurus rexes* once walked the Earth.

Dead as a dodo?

The dodo was a flightless bird discovered in 1507 – but, by 1681, it was extinct. However, there may be hope for this ancient creature.

Scientists at the Mauritian Wildlife Foundation signed a deal with a US company to try to bring the dodo back from extinction. Today, its closest living relative is the Nicobar pigeon. Scientists aim to use the pigeon's **DNA** to recreate dodo DNA.

CREATURE
FEATURES

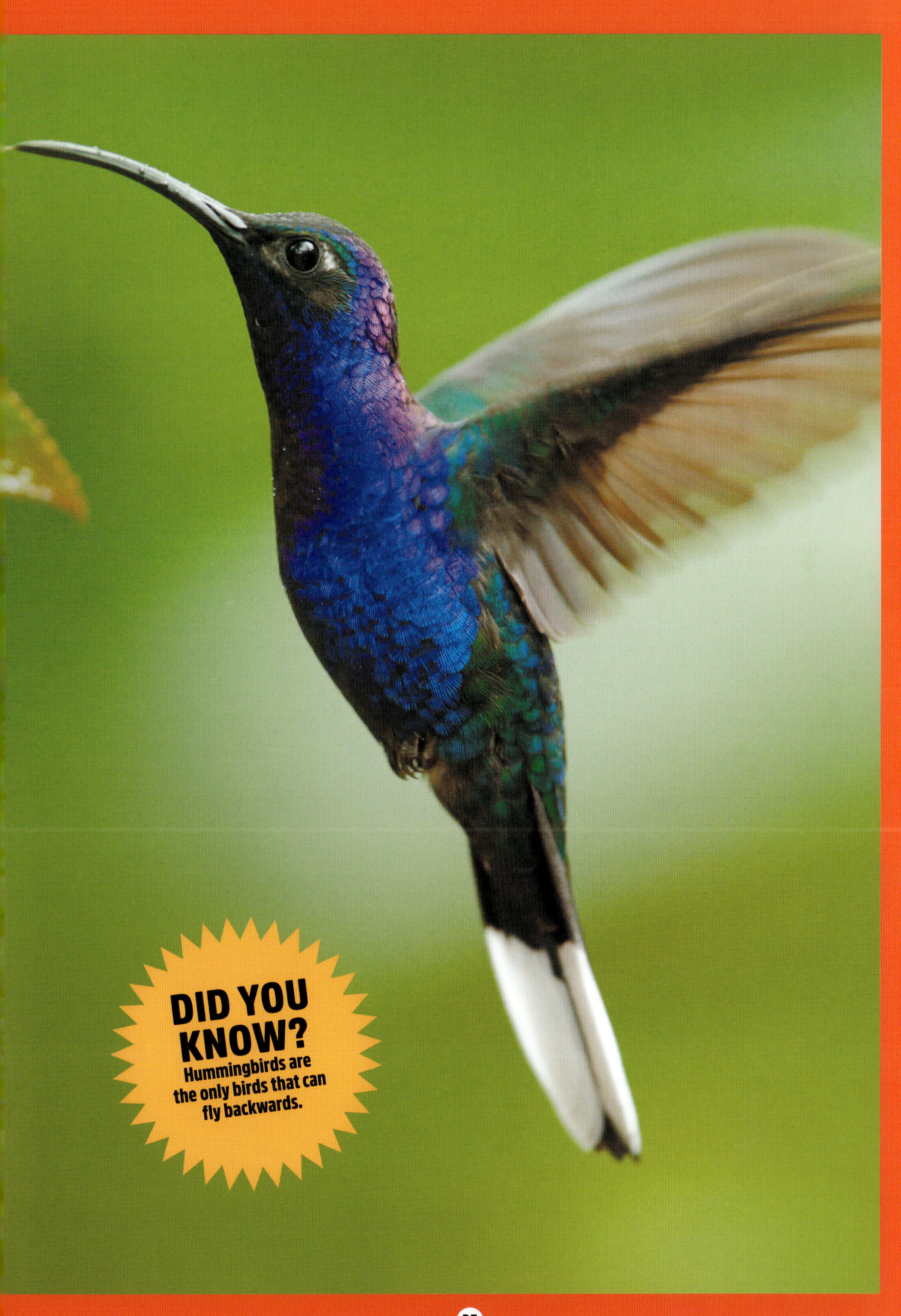

DID YOU
KNOW?
Hummingbirds are
the only birds that can
fly backwards.

BRILLIANT BIRDS

Siren-song fools police

A bird was heard copying the sounds of police sirens in Oxfordshire, UK.

When Inspector Hills noticed a strange noise, he thought a police car's siren was broken. Hills said, "I came outside and looked up into the trees, and I could see the bird mimicking the sirens in a really professional way."

The inspector added that he wasn't planning to arrest the bird unless it started wearing a police uniform.

Animal identifier: birds

Skeleton:	Internal	☑
	External	☐
Skin:	Hairy	☐
	Smooth	☐
	Scaly	☐
	Feathery	☑
Breathing:	In water	☐
	In air	☑
Blood:	Cold	☐
	Warm	☑
Babies:	Live	☐
	From hard-shelled eggs	☑
	From soft-shelled eggs	☐

COPY CAT CALLS

Many birds, including starlings and crows, can recreate human-made sounds quite convincingly.

An amazingly artistic bird

An injured bird reinvented himself as a painter.

After a wing injury left Ferrisburgh the kestrel unable to fly, staff at a nature centre introduced him to painting. He took to it like a bird to a branch and has even helped lead an art class for visitors.

Some of Ferrisburgh's paintings are being sold to support the nature centre.

Cockerel catches a ride

Jessica Matthews, from Aston-on-Trent, UK, helped to **rehome** a cockerel after it flew into her car.

She spotted the bird wandering along a country lane. When she opened the car window to check it was ok, the cockerel flew into her car and made himself comfortable on the passenger seat.

"He just didn't want to get out," said Matthews. The cockerel was rehomed the next day, but Matthews wasn't entirely relieved. "It was really hard to give him away because he was really nice," she said.

Suspected snooper flies free

A pigeon accused of spying for China has been cleared of wrongdoing and released.

When the unlucky bird was captured in India, rings on its legs appeared to feature a message in a Chinese language. Detectives decided it was best to keep the animal under lock and key.

Further investigations took eight months, but eventually revealed that the bird was an escaped Taiwanese racing pigeon. As it wasn't up to any sinister activities, the pigeon was granted its freedom.

Pigeons versus birds of prey

Officials in Barcelona, Spain, are aiming to keep pigeons under control. They say there are twice as many pigeons as there should be in some areas, so are **trialling** the use of eagles and falcons to scare pigeons away.

Real OR rubbish?

Pigeon parachute

An 80-year-old pigeon parachute has been found by a family in the UK when clearing out a loft.

During the Second World War (1939–1945), the British Army used carrier pigeons to deliver secret messages to soldiers in France. Pigeons in cages with parachutes were released from low-flying planes. When they were found, another message could be attached to the pigeon, which would then fly home. The pigeon parachute is now on display in a museum.

Is this real or have we released a lie?*

* **Real!** Pigeons were equipped with little parachutes and used during the Second World War to deliver messages.

MARVELLOUS MAMMALS

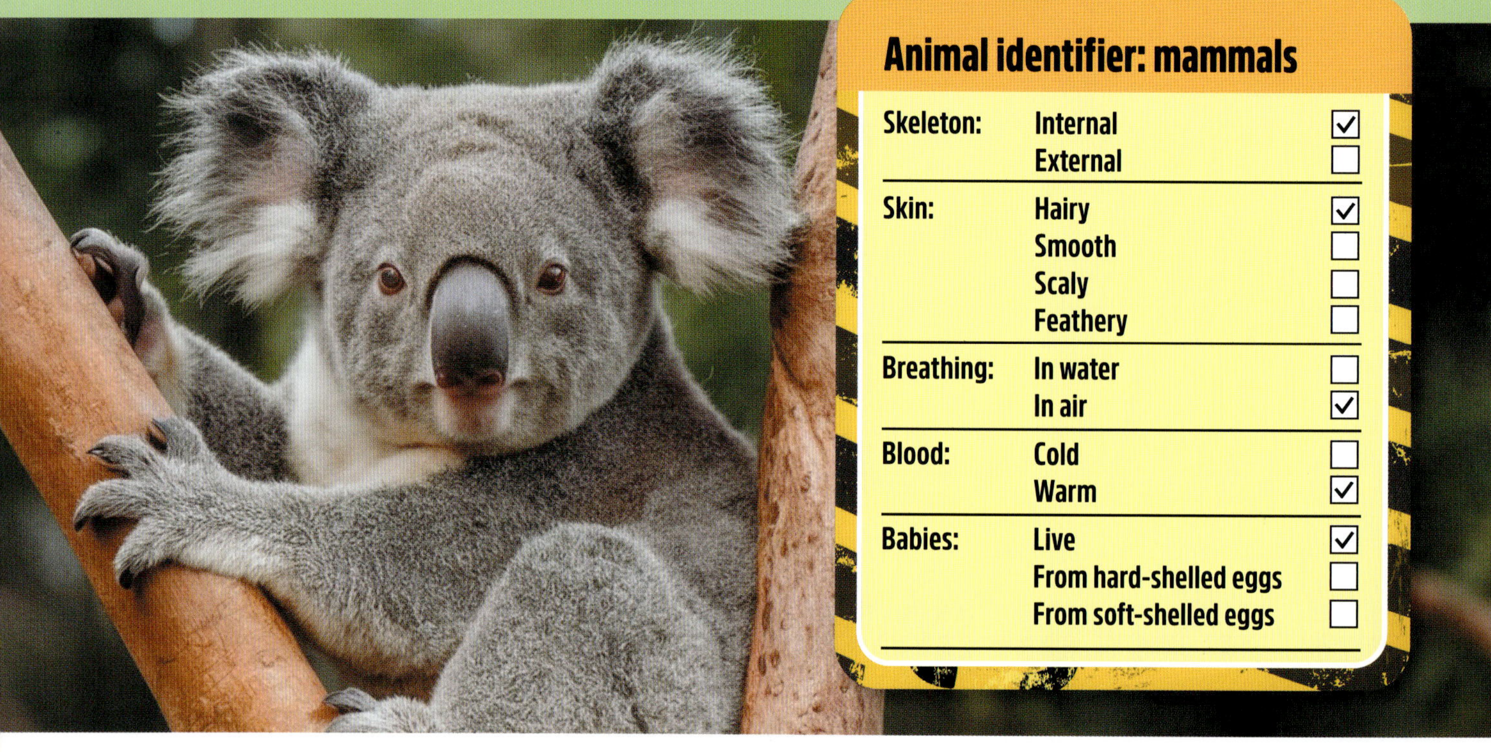

Animal identifier: mammals

Skeleton:	Internal	☑
	External	☐
Skin:	Hairy	☑
	Smooth	☐
	Scaly	☐
	Feathery	☐
Breathing:	In water	☐
	In air	☑
Blood:	Cold	☐
	Warm	☑
Babies:	Live	☑
	From hard-shelled eggs	☐
	From soft-shelled eggs	☐

Many mammals glow in certain light

Many animals, like jellyfish and scorpions, glow under UV light. Surprisingly, at least 125 species of mammals also glow, including koalas, wombats, and leopards. Their fur, skin, spines, and nails may shine, especially in lighter-colored animals, such as the white stripes of zebras. This glowing is more common in nocturnal animals. The reason for this glow is not clear. It might help animals see each other in low light, but it could also make them easier for predators to spot.

COLOURFUL CREATURES
Platypuses glow blue-green under UV light, while some rodents glow pink.

A house-proud mouse

When Rodney Holbrook noticed that objects left out in his shed were often tidied away overnight, he set up a camera. To his surprise, the secret cleaner was a little mouse. The furry creature gathered corks, clothes pegs and screws, and tidied them into a tray.

Holbrook, who calls his little friend "Welsh Tidy Mouse", said, "I don't bother to tidy up now, as I know he will see to it."

Why are sloths so slow?

Sloths need to save energy because their stomachs digest low-energy leaves slowly. They also have poor eyesight, so climbing quickly would be tricky. Their slow speed allows algae to grow on their fur, too, meaning they're **camouflaged** from predators.

Spotlight: Rats

A rat-friendly city

Dutch scientists have argued that Amsterdam should be a rat-friendly city. Despite their dirty reputation, rats are actually very clean, and scientist Maite van Gerwen believes their image problem is unfair.

"Why do we want certain animals around us and not others?" she asked. The team suggested having feeding areas in parks so people could get to know rats a bit better.

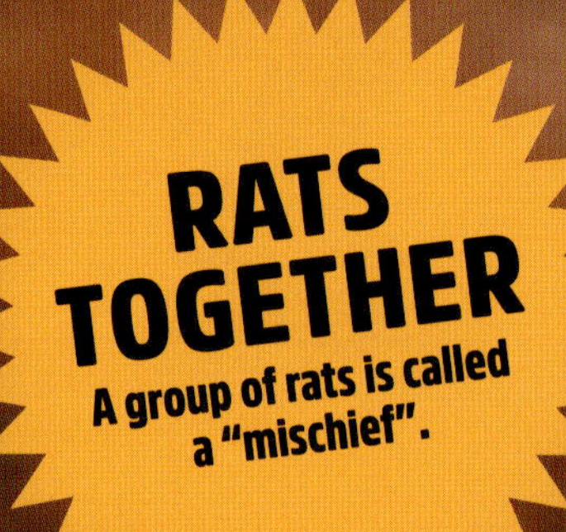

Rats may use imagination to navigate

Agroup of scientists looked into whether animals can use the power of imagination. The scientists put the rats into **treadmill** balls that showed **virtual reality** scenes – like a video game. The rats received treats for moving to specific locations in the games using the treadmills, and their brain signals were recorded.

The scientists then disconnected the treadmills but continued to monitor the rats' brain signals. The rats were still able to navigate, using just their thoughts. The researchers thought this meant that the rats were creating images of the area in their minds using their imaginations.

The hidden language of rats

When rats are with their friends, they signal how happy they are using squeaks too high-pitched for humans to hear.

Scientists in Israel created tiny microphones that could pick up these squeaks. They attached the microphones to rats' noses and listened to the rodents squeaking with joy.

The microphones also picked up a low-pitched, soft squeak that rats never make near humans. Scientists have yet to work out what this mystery squeak means.

REMARKABLE REPTILES

It's raining iguanas

During very cold weather in Florida, US, residents had to prepare themselves for iguanas falling from trees.

These lizards find it hard to control their body temperatures in the cold. To cope, they relax their muscles – and can sometimes lose their grip on branches.

Animal identifier: reptiles

Skeleton:	Internal	☑
	External	☐
Skin:	Hairy	☐
	Smooth	☐
	Scaly	☑
	Feathery	☐
Breathing:	In water	☐
	In air	☑
Blood:	Cold	☑
	Warm	☐
Babies:	Live	☑
	From hard-shelled eggs	☐
	From soft-shelled eggs	☐

Masters of disguise

Colour-changing chameleons can make special chemicals and rearrange **cells** in their skin to hide against their surroundings. This can depend on their mood, too: their colours become brighter when they're happy.

Alligators were frozen in ponds.

Alligators à la mode

During a cold snap, people came across a shocking sight at the Swamp Park in North Carolina, US. Alligators lay motionless in frozen ponds, suspended in ice, like solid "gatorcicles".

Surprisingly, the reptiles were not dead: alligators can become still to survive harsh weather.

Each inanimate animal had left its snout sticking up through the ice so it could breathe. "Think of it as a cute little danger snorkel," said a park employee.

Real OR rubbish?

Police hunt croc on the loose

A pet crocodile escaped from its pool in Buckinghamshire, UK, and police had to hunt it down.

Months of heavy rainfall had filled the pool with so much water that the weight broke the tank and the crocodile was able to get out. It made its way into a drainage ditch and swam out into the countryside.

The owner didn't notice the animal had escaped until feeding time. A member of the public spotted it lurking in floodwater and called the police, who brought the croc home.

Is this true or have we let loose a lie?*

*__Rubbish!__ Some pranksters stuck a plastic crocodile head in a big pool of floodwater. Thames Valley Police officers retrieved the head and reported, "The croc is now with us at the police station."

Spotlight: Snakes

A spectacular snake

Unbelievable species are still being discovered worldwide, including a snake that could be the largest in the world. The northern green anaconda was spotted in the Amazon rainforest during filming for TV show *Pole to Pole*.

Scientists found a female anaconda that was 6.3 metres long. Local people have reported seeing even bigger ones – measuring more than 7.5 metres and weighing around 500 kilograms.

FACT FOCUS — Life-sssssavvers

Although some snake venoms can be deadly, others help us. It may sound surprising, but venom can be used to treat heart problems.

Dr Zoltan Takacs, an expert in poisons and venoms, says the jararaca pit viper snake has saved "more human lives than any other animal in the history of mankind".

"Male" snake has 14 babies

A snake that people thought was male surprised her owners by having 14 babies.

Ronaldo, a Brazilian rainbow boa constrictor, was living at City of Portsmouth College, UK. Staff there were stunned as Ronaldo hadn't had contact with another snake in nine years.

Some animals can give birth without mates, but in rainbow boas it has only been known to happen a few times. "We couldn't believe our eyes," staff member Amanda McLeod said.

A baby rainbow boa

BYGONE BEASTS

The oldest-known word for dragon is ušum-gal, which means 'big snake' in ancient Sumerian.

AMAZING AMPHIBIANS

Adopt an axolotl

A**campaign** was relaunched by Mexico's National Autonomous University to help save the axolotl.

The creature's natural habitat has been under threat due to human action and **climate change**. They're also traded illegally as pets – so the team created a way for them to become "pets" without harm.

As part of the university's AdoptAxolotl campaign, for a small fee people can "virtually adopt" one of the creatures. For a little less, they can buy it dinner.

Animal identifier: amphibians

Skeleton:	Internal	☑
	External	☐
Skin:	Hairy	☐
	Smooth	☐
	Scaly	☑
	Feathery	☐
Breathing:	In water	☐
	In air	☑
Blood:	Cold	☑
	Warm	☐
Babies:	Live	☑
	From hard-shelled eggs	☐
	From soft-shelled eggs	☐

A tiny toad

Scientists have revealed what they believe is the smallest **vertebrate** in the world. The Brazilian flea toad is found in only two forested hills in southern Bahia, Brazil. The rare creatures average a tiny 7 millimetres in length: two of them could sit on an average adult's little fingernail.

Saving the salamanders

In the Watauga River in North Carolina, US, scientists have been making big conservation efforts. They needed to react to a big environmental change: a **dam** was due to be removed in an effort to make the river healthier.

However, the process could have damaged the rare hellbender salamanders that lived in the river. The team caught the salamanders and moved them downstream to keep them safe.

NICKNAMES

Hellbenders have a surprising number of nicknames, including "snot otter", "mud devil" and "lasagna lizard".

Spotlight: Frogs

World's first amphibian pollinators

Scientists in Brazil believe they have discovered a frog that **pollinates** plants. Before the discovery, no amphibians were known to be pollinators.

Most frogs eat insects and other small creatures, but some include plants in their diet. Scientists noticed *Xenohyla truncata*, tiny yellow-orange tree frogs in Brazil, plunging into the flowers of Brazilian milk fruit trees to drink their nectar.

Afterwards, they had pollen stuck to their bodies. When they hopped to another flower, the frogs took the pollen with them.

"This was amazing," said researcher Carlos Henrique de-Oliveira-Nogueira.

FACT FOCUS The first redheads

Frogs may hold the title of the world's first redheads.

Scientists have discovered the earliest known record of phaeomelanin, the colour chemical that makes people's hair red, in frog fossils from 10 million years ago. The discovery will help scientists understand how some animals developed red colours over time.

The search for a quacking frog

A Noa-Dihing music frog

Scientists have discovered a new species of frog in India that has a call like a duck's quack. They first heard the unusual sound near the Noa-Dihing river in a region of northern India called Arunachal Pradesh. The researchers carried out night-time searches to find the frogs.

When they were located, the teams had another surprise: they found that the male Noa-Dihing music frogs made circular pits out of grass, which they used like private pools.

FABULOUS FISH

Little fish making a big noise

It may be just 12 millimetres long, but a fish species called the *Danionella cerebrum* makes a noise as loud as a gunshot or a **bulldozer**.

Scientists in Berlin, Germany, investigated fish tanks in their laboratories to find the source of some very noisy clicks. Researchers think it is a way for the fish to communicate with each other.

Verity Cook, one of the lab's scientists, said, "I couldn't find another animal of this size that makes sounds this loud."

Sharks solve an ocean mystery

Seagrass is an essential source of shelter, food and oxygen. It also helps prevent climate change by storing **carbon**.

To shed light on how much seagrass there is in ocean depths we can't reach, scientists turned to tiger sharks. Sharks were fitted with cameras and **tracking tags**, which showed they swam through around 65,000 square kilometres of seagrass near the Bahamas: much more than expected.

The findings increased the amount of seagrass known to exist by 41%.

Parrotfish pose problems

Off the coast of Croatia, the Mediterranean parrotfish is causing problems. The parrotfish is one of many species that have spread there because of climate change.

These "invasive species" harm the environment by eating food the local fish need. Unfortunately, fishermen don't reduce numbers because they can't sell parrotfish. One said, "The local population won't eat this new fish."

OTHER UNDERSEA SPECIES

Fish share the seas with some truly amazing animals.

Sweet octopus dreams

When octopuses sleep, they can change their skin's colour and **texture**. Researchers think this could mean they're dreaming.

Studies show that octopuses have two types of sleep, called "active" and "quiet" sleep. During active sleep, their skin changes and their arms and eyes move. This behaviour is like that of mammals, including humans, during sleep stages when they commonly dream.

Strange species

A team of scientists spotted some unusual creatures 4–5 kilometres below the surface of the Pacific Ocean.

These included a see-through sea cucumber (a long jelly-like creature), which the scientists called the "unicumber", and a sea pig nicknamed the "Barbie pig" due to its bright pink colour. The creature has lots of legs and tiny feet, and crawls across the sea bed to find food.

Experts believe some of the creatures had never been seen before.

All head and no limbs

Sea stars have puzzled scientists for years: there is no obvious place where their heads end and the rest of their bodies begin.

A study has now revealed that, instead of starfish being a head with five limbs, the arrangement of **genes** shows they're actually one big head with limb-like extensions.

Laurent Formery, who led the study, said starfish are best described as "just a head crawling along the sea floor".

FACT FOCUS Reach for the stars

Sea anemones may look like plants, but they're animals. Snakelocks anemones are the first known animals to follow sunlight like plants do: their tentacles follow the Sun's movement.

Spotlight: Crabs

Animal identifier: crustaceans

Bones:	Yes	☐
	No	☑
Skin:	Hairy	☐
	Smooth	☑
	Scaly	☐
	Feathery	☐
Breathing:	In water	☐
	In air	☑
Blood:	Cold	☑
	Warm	☐
Babies:	Live, without shells	☐
	From hard-shelled eggs	☐
	From soft-shelled eggs	☑

Giant crab's unusual hairdo

A couple was amazed to find a stylish spiny spider crab washed up on a beach in north Wales.

"With his little hairdo of mussels stuck to him, it was very, very fascinating," they said.

An expert from Anglesey Sea Zoo explained that crab shells make good "anchor points" for mussels to cling to against the waves.

Real OR rubbish?

Crabs judge joke competition

Crabs are not known for their sense of humour, but a panel made up of crabs chose the winner of the World's Funniest Crab Joke competition.

School children and comedians looked at the entries and chose the best four jokes. These were written on pieces of paper and presented to the crab judges, who picked their favourite one.

Is this real, or is there something fishy about this tale?*

* **Real!** The winning joke was this:

A man walks into a restaurant with a crab under his arm and says, "Do you make crab cakes?"
The manager answers, "Yes, we do."
"Good," says the man, "because it's his birthday."

INCREDIBLE INSECTS

Skeleton:	Internal	☐
	External	☑
Skin:	Hairy	☐
	Smooth	☐
	Scaly	☑
	Feathery	☐
Breathing:	In water	☐
	In air	☑
Blood:	Cold	☑
	Warm	☐
Babies:	Live	☐
	From hard-shelled eggs	☐
	From soft-shelled eggs	☑

DID YOU KNOW?

Like crustaceans, insects have exoskeletons. Beetles have very hard, smooth ones. Flies' exoskeletons are soft and hairy. Moths and butterflies have tiny scales as exoskeletons.

Monster mystery's sweet solution

Shortly after watching the film *Monsters, Inc.* three-year-old Saylor Class complained that she could hear monsters in her bedroom wall. Her parents thought it was just her imagination.

After a while, though, Saylor's mum noticed bees swarming outside their house and called a beekeeper to investigate. The beekeeper found around 60,000 bees in a giant hive in the attic. They had made so much honey that it damaged the house's electrical wiring. The bees were taken away to a **sanctuary** to be kept safe.

The truth about caterpillars' "legs"

Caterpillars may seem to have 16 legs, but only six are real: the others are limbs called "prolegs". Caterpillars use them to get about more easily while they eat as much as possible. When they become butterflies, they eat less, so prolegs aren't needed.

What is the strongest animal at the zoo?

A zookeeper told us that when you think about strong animals, you might think of huge mammals like elephants. However, if you compare body size to strength, the strongest members of the animal kingdom can actually come in small sizes.

Leafcutter ants can carry 10 times their body weight, and dung beetles can roll balls of poo that are 50 times their body weight. The insect world may be small, but it's mighty.

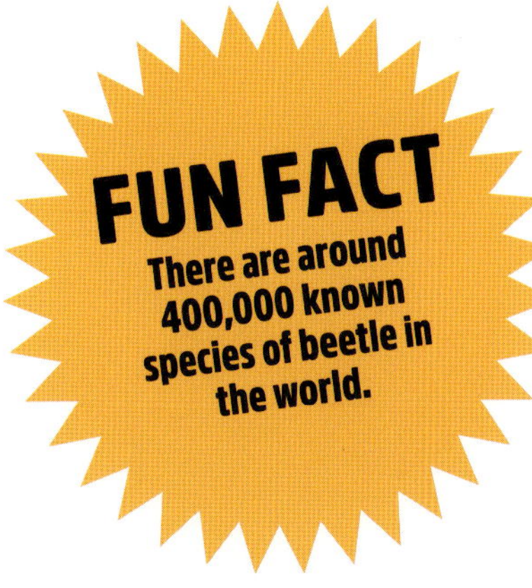

Slug mail to help farmers

Scientists studying ways to make crops resist pests have been collecting slugs for their research.

In a creative approach to gathering specimens, researchers provided special "slug scout" packs with containers, mailing supplies, and habitat-building guides to help people capture these garden pests.

This research matters because slugs cause around £43.5 million in crop damage across the UK annually. By understanding these creatures better, scientists hope to develop more effective ways to protect plants.

Grey Field Slugs destroy crops all over northern Europe.

An ancient creepy crawly

The largest-ever fossil of a giant millipede was found in 2018 on a beach in Northumberland, UK. This particular example of *Arthropleura* would have been as big as a car and dates from more than 100 million years before the dinosaurs.

Super soil heroes

Scientists know earthworms help plants to grow. Worms make soil healthier by eating dead plants and producing **nutrients** from them. They also create tunnels that help plants to grow roots and keep water underground.

To investigate the fuller impact of earthworms on farming, researchers compared global maps of worm populations with maps showing soil quality and crop growth. They revealed that earthworms help to grow 6.5% of the world's grain (such as rice, corn and wheat), making them one of the world's greatest grain producers.

Other creatures in the soil probably have a positive impact, too. Researcher Steven Fonte believes this highlights the need for more **biodiversity** studies.

Spotlight: Snails

The dangers of snail mail

A post box in Lewdown, UK, was overrun for over a year by snails with an appetite for letters. The postal service said that, despite daily efforts to remove the snails, the "very determined" creatures always returned.

The post office finally taped a sign to the post box, warning that letters might not arrive "without some nibble marks around the edges".

Saving snails

Ecologists in France have been rescuing Quimper snails by hand. The snails had to be moved from their homes to keep them safe from building work on a new public transport system.

Quimper snails only live in certain parts of France and Spain, and conservationists hope that moving them somewhere else will help to save the species from extinction.

What is the rarest animal at a zoo?

A zookeeper told us that it's *Partula* rosea, a small pink snail from the Pacific Island of Huahine. These snails were wiped out in the wild 30 years ago by the rosy wolf snail, a non-native species put on the island to eat giant African land snails.

At one point, there were only 79 *Partula rosea* snails in the world, all protected in zoos. Scientists are working to recover the species and release them back into the wild.

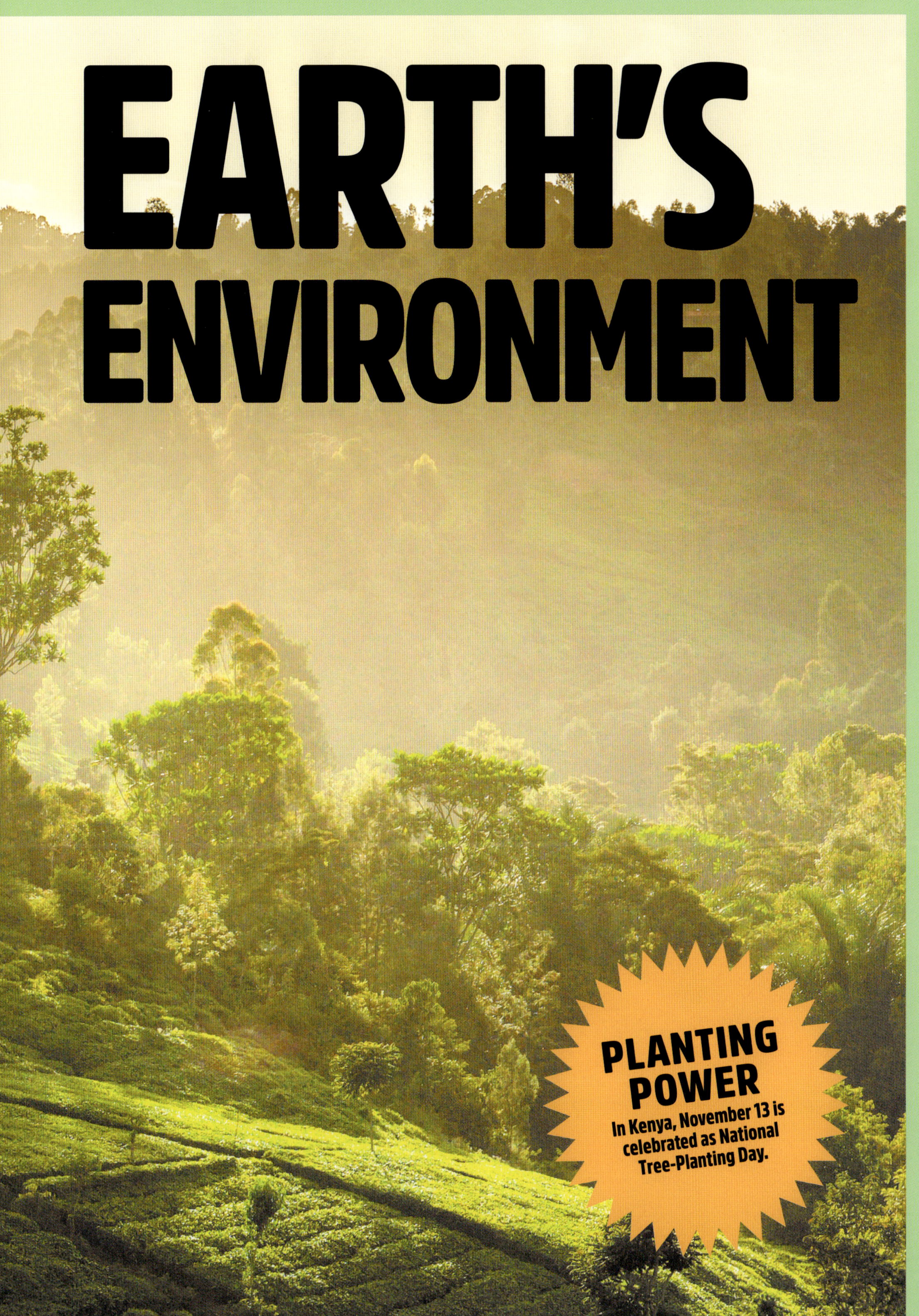

EARTH'S ENVIRONMENT
PLANTING POWER
In Kenya, November 13 is celebrated as National Tree-Planting Day.

GOOD NEWS STORIES

We live in a difficult time for the environment. However, despite the challenges for our planet, there are lots of news stories for nature lovers.

Climate plan agreed

The small Pacific island nation of Tuvalu has an agreement with Australia to protect it from climate change. Each year, 280 Tuvaluans can move to Australia, and Australia gives £8.8 million to help adapt to rising sea levels.

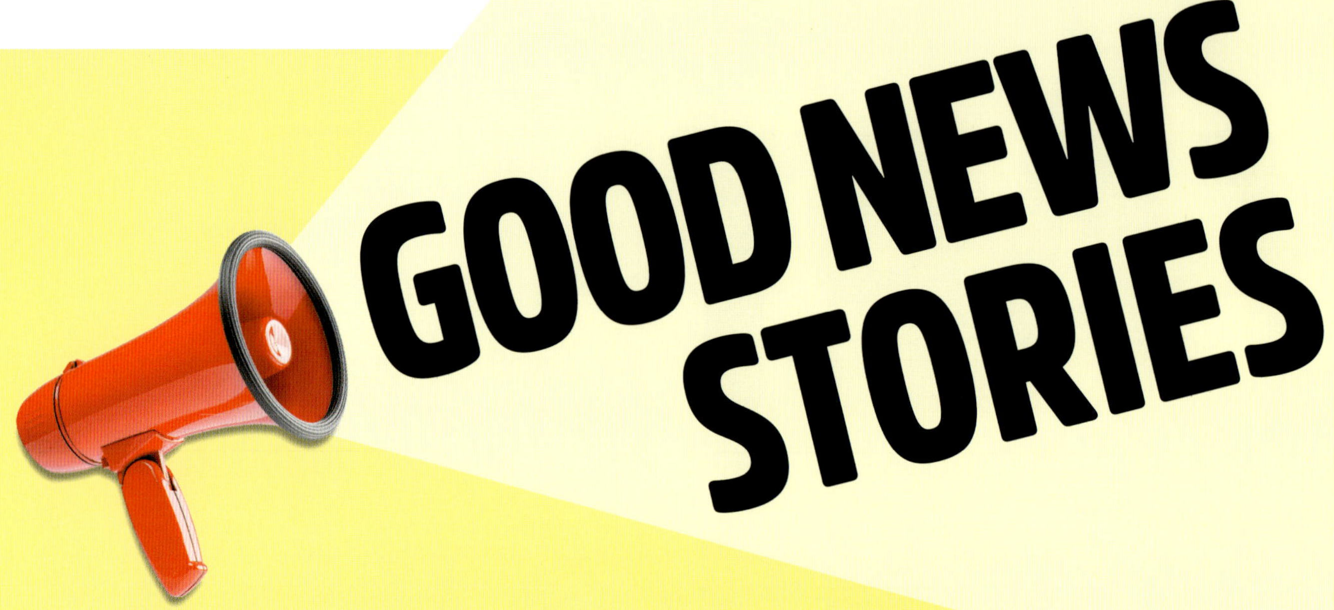

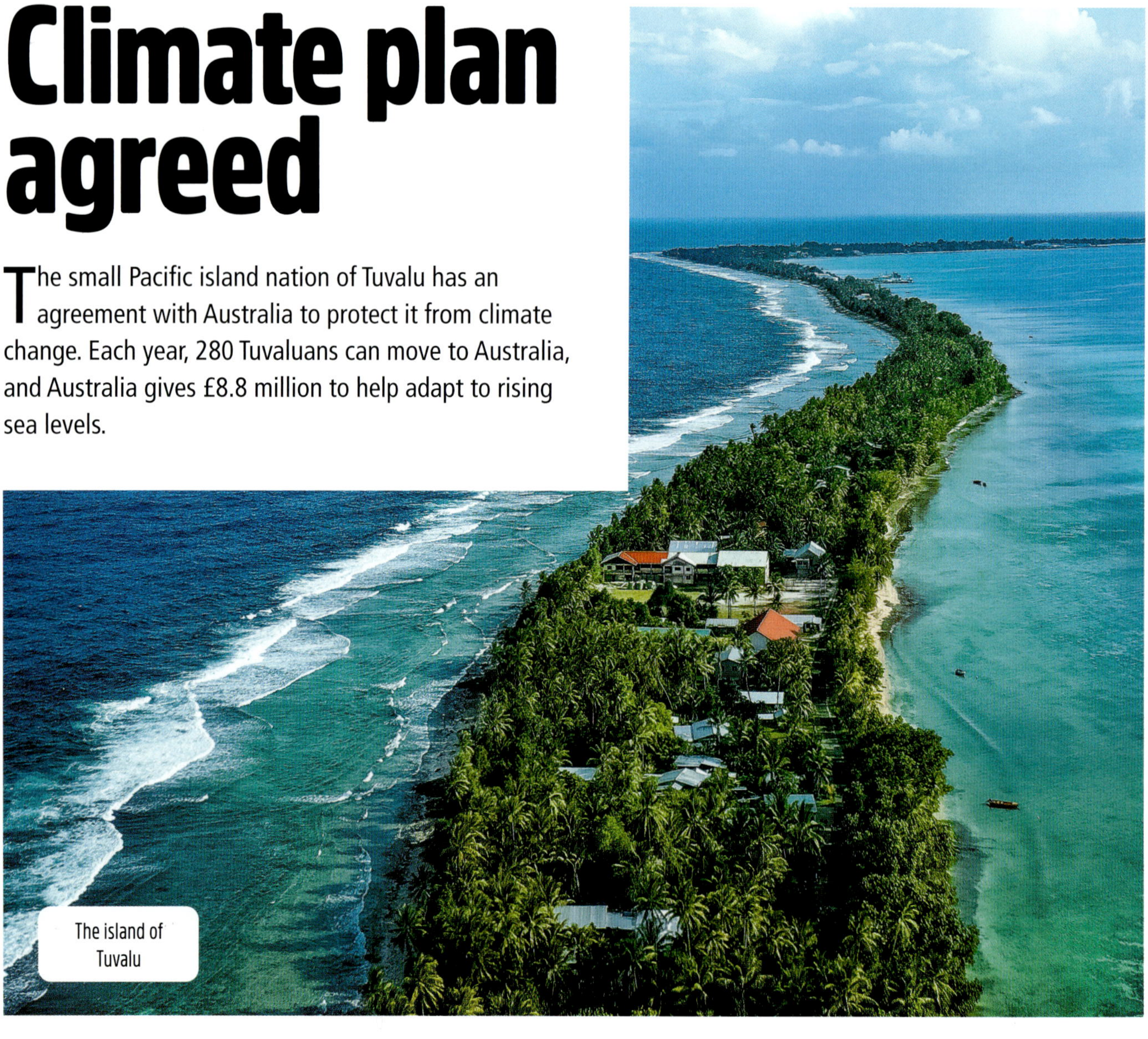

The island of Tuvalu

What's happening with climate change?

On Earth, climate change is being sped up by human activity such as burning **fossil fuels**.

In most areas, this has meant rising temperatures. A lot of ice has melted, and therefore sea levels have risen. Climate change is also linked to extreme weather such as floods, **droughts** and violent storms.

Crackdown on short flights

To reduce air pollution from planes, France has banned domestic flights on routes that can be travelled by train in less than 2.5 hours.

This ban took effect in 2023, initially affecting three major routes between Paris and other French cities. The government allowed exceptions for connecting flights, ensuring travellers could still reach international destinations.

Rare mammals rediscovered

More than 60 years after it was last spotted in 1961, researchers from Oxford University, UK, caught a long-beaked echidna on camera. The discovery was made on the very last day of their **expedition** in Indonesia.

The Gould's mouse was thought to have been extinct for 125 years, but scientists found it had survived on an Australian island. At first, it was mistaken for a Shark Bay mouse.

MAKING A DIFFERENCE

There are many countries across the world that are working hard to make positive changes to help the environment.

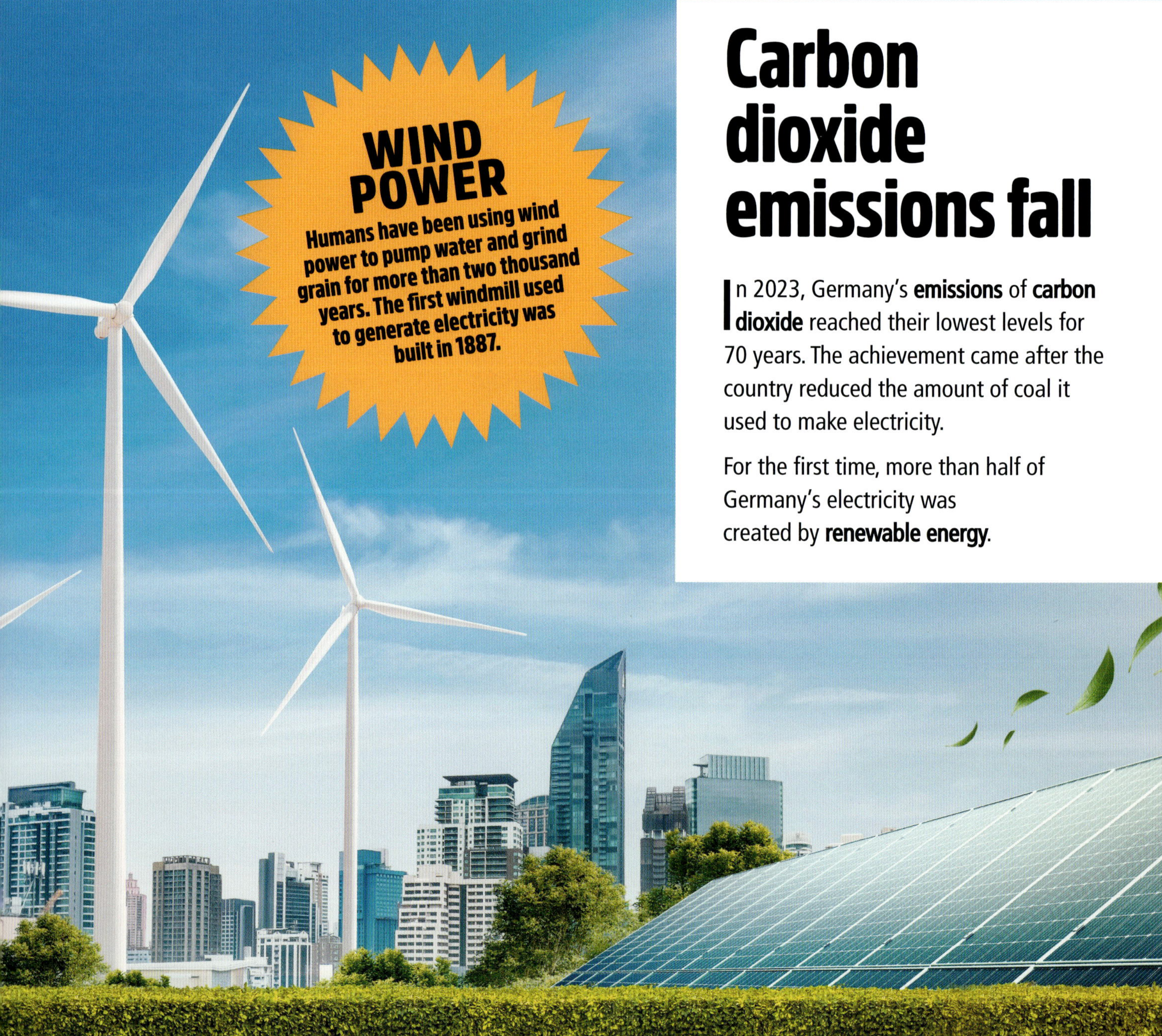

Carbon dioxide emissions fall

In 2023, Germany's **emissions** of **carbon dioxide** reached their lowest levels for 70 years. The achievement came after the country reduced the amount of coal it used to make electricity.

For the first time, more than half of Germany's electricity was created by **renewable energy**.

Tiny forests spring up

Tiny forests, called Miyawaki forests or "pocket forests", were invented by a Japanese scientist called Akira Miyawaki. They feature fast-growing trees and shrubs in small areas.

The idea is now spreading westwards: New York City, US, planned its first pocket forest in 2023 – a small patch of land covering 250 square metres to be home to more than 1,000 plants.

Plans for New York's forest

Waging war on plastic pollution

After years of work, the state of New York, US, succeeded in taking legal action against PepsiCo, which makes lots of food and drink products, over plastic pollution. The state's lawyers said that surveys along the Buffalo River found lots of plastic waste from products made by the company. In a statement, PepsiCo said that it's "serious about plastic reduction".

A study found that Nigeria produces more than 2.5 million tonnes of plastic waste each year, with 130,000 tonnes ending up in rivers and lakes.

However, the Nigerian government has announced a ban on single-use plastic products (such as straws and plastic bottles) in the city of Lagos. Officials also announced plans to expand the ban countrywide in 2025.

HUMANS
HARMING THE WORLD

The environment needs lots of care. We all need to do what we can to stop damaging it, reduce human waste and preserve animal habitats.

Venezuela's final glacier lost

Venezuela's last remaining **glacier** has melted because of climate change.

La Corona, also known as the Humboldt glacier, is 5,000 metres up in the Andes mountains. It is now so small that scientists have reclassified it as an ice "field".

Five other glaciers in Venezuela have also melted away in the last century.

Ferocious flooding across Africa

After heavy rainfall started at the end of November 2023, the African continent experienced its worst flooding in 60 years. It affected homes, schools and hospitals, and meant 280,000 families had to move.

More than 20,000 families had to leave their homes because of flooding in several areas of Kenya. Rail services carrying cargo to and from Mombasa were also affected following a landslide.

Unusually heavy rain led to floods in Somalia. Almost 700,000 people's homes were destroyed and over 100 people were killed. Before the floods, Somalia had been experiencing a drought that lasted for several years.

The government delivered food and boats by plane to help people in the areas that were worst hit.

Houses submerged in water during heavy floods in Kenya

Wildfires spread

Forest fires have always occurred in Chile during dry summers, but the 2024 fires were far worse than ever before. Climate change has made fires more extreme in the region. During a massive fire near Valparaiso, thousands of homes were destroyed and at least 112 people died. The country's president, Gabriel Boric, explained that unusually high temperatures, strong winds, and very dry air made the fires extremely dangerous and hard to stop.

Pollution closes classrooms

Some schools in Delhi, India have been forced to shut in winter because of the city's bad air quality. In 2023, levels of pollution reached nearly 100 times the official "healthy" level set by the World Health Organisation.

In winter, Delhi is often polluted by smoke that largely comes from farmers burning old crops ready to plant new ones. This is often made worse by lots of fireworks being set off during the Diwali festival.

Extreme heat empties schools

Some schools in South Sudan now have to close in summer because of extreme hot weather.

Children were advised to stay indoors because temperatures reached 45°C. In March 2024, the heat also caused **power cuts** in parts of South Sudan's capital, Juba.

Reservoir shrinks

The Al Massira **reservoir**, which provides fresh water for some of Morocco's biggest cities, is shrinking. Scientists say it contains just 3% of the water it held nine years ago. Six years of high temperatures and long periods of drought have made the situation worse.

GARDENS LIKE GREENHOUSES

Some rising temperature stories may seem to be good news, but big changes like these can have unpredictable effects.

FACT FOCUS

Nature's new risks

As weather patterns change, the growth cycle of plants changes too. Warmer temperatures mean blossoms and fruit appear early, and may die off before insects can pollinate flowers or other animals can eat fruit and spread seeds.

When new and different kinds of plants grow somewhere, they can be a danger to existing natural life. They can use up **resources** for other plants and often block light. They even risk poisoning animals.

Tropical jungle in the back garden

Scientist Dr Simon Olpin has been growing a tropical jungle in his garden in Sheffield, UK. It contains more than 100 species of tropical plants, including eight-metre-tall palm trees.

Gigantic rhododendron blooms

A plant known as "Big Rhodey" in West Sussex, UK, has bloomed a month earlier than usual because of far wetter, warmer weather.

Big Rhodey is more than 120 years old, and was named because of its huge growth until now: it's around 80 metres long and nearly 30 metres tall.

A rhododendron

Backyard plant goes bananas

A banana plant in London, UK, has started producing fruit for the first time in ten years. Bananas typically grow in hot and tropical regions, like Southeast Asia, South America and Africa. However, this London plant is flourishing in the wet summer weather.

TRACKED CHANGES

Experts have been uncovering hard evidence of ways the world has warmed – even before humans sped up the process.

Ancient flowers show changes

Scientists have compared modern plant life near Bologna, Italy, to a huge collection of dried flowers from 1551–1586.

They found that the variety of species has increased, but numbers of local species have fallen. Plants native to far warmer areas, including South America, became ten times more common. If they can survive, temperatures must have risen, likely killing the local flowers.

Flowers of the Bologna landscape

Trees reveal ancient weather

Researchers have succeeded in using fossilised tree rings to study temperatures over thousands of years. The number of rings inside the trunk shows how many years the tree has been alive.

Tree growth changes in different weather conditions, researchers could track temperatures every summer from the year 1 CE. This confirmed that summer 2023 was the hottest in 2,000 years, proving that temperatures have risen continuously.

Teeth show why giant apes died

Experts have long known that temperatures rose between 700,000 and 600,000 years ago. Over many years, forests became drier, and fruit trees died out.

To discover how this may have led to the extinction of ancient giant apes called *Gigantopithecus blacki* (referred to as "Giganto" by researchers), scientists compared the apes' fossilised teeth with the teeth of surviving Chinese orangutans.

Tooth shapes suggest that when fruit trees died out, orangutans ate soft leaves and flowers that grew high up in the remaining trees. Giganto teeth were worn away by tough, chewy foods.

Gigantos could grow to three metres tall and weigh up to 300 kilograms. Researchers think they were too big to climb trees, so had to eat dry bark and twigs. These were not nutritious – so Giganto died out.

Scientists say these findings will help them learn more about how apes cope with changing climates.

An artist's impression of Giganto

NATURAL DEFENCES

In the search for ways to combat climate change, some scientists suggest we turn to nature for help.

The ragworm is just one creature that lives in coastal mud.

Digging up the secrets of mud

Scientists in Scotland are investigating creatures found in mud on UK coastlines, that could work against climate change.

Many mud-burrowing creatures feed on tiny **organisms** like **algae** and plankton. When these organisms die in the sea, they release carbon dioxide. However, the mud-dwellers pull many of them down into the sea bed, trapping the gas. The scientists are measuring which of the 200 species in the mud are best at this.

The researcher leading the project says, "It couldn't be a more important time to work out how we can best utilise nature's power to lock carbon away."

FACT FOCUS Old trees fight new changes

Trees absorb carbon dioxide – and, scientists say, letting forests grow old could take 226 billion tonnes of carbon out of the air. "Old growth" forests contain a variety of trees that haven't been disturbed by humans. These larger trees mean more leaves per area, so they can absorb more gas.

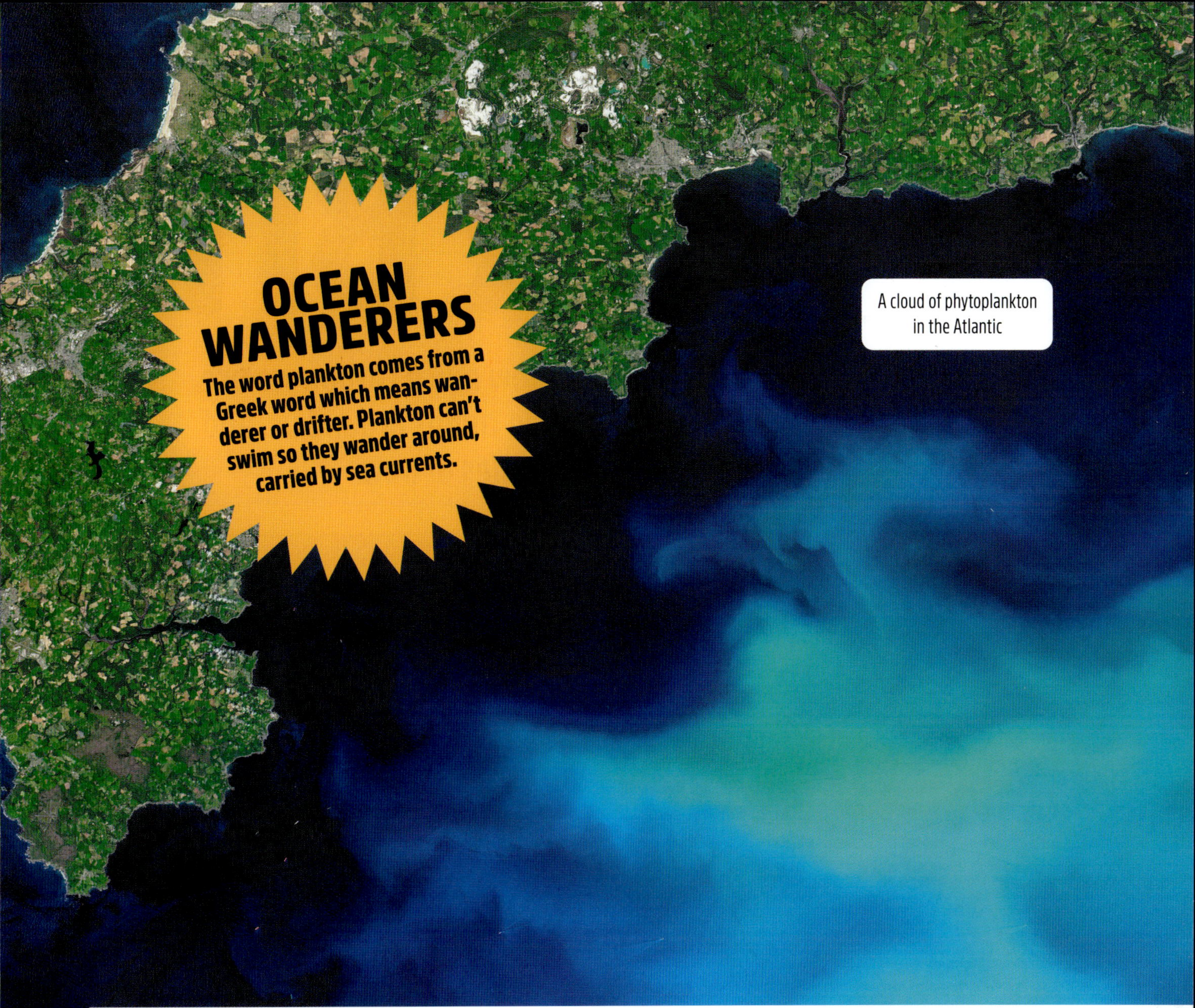

A cloud of phytoplankton in the Atlantic

OCEAN WANDERERS

The word plankton comes from a Greek word which means wanderer or drifter. Plankton can't swim so they wander around, carried by sea currents.

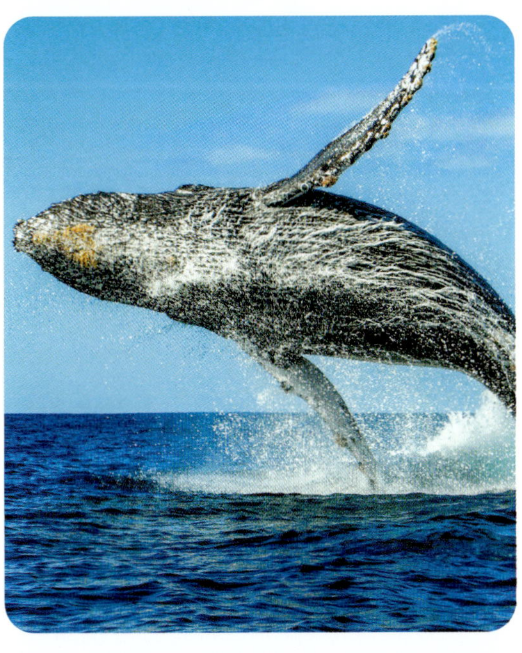

Whales slow climate change

Whales play an important role in removing carbon dioxide from the atmosphere.

Tiny sea creatures called phytoplankton absorb even more carbon from the air than trees do. Whale poo provides lots of the nutrients that these lifeforms need.

Whales' enormous bodies also store many tonnes of carbon. When they die and sink to the ocean floor, that carbon is locked away so it can't become carbon dioxide in the air for many years.

Do **YOUR BIT!**

There are ways we can all help to reduce how much carbon we use. We can repair, repurpose, reuse and recycle things around us, and reduce our waste. Here are just a few examples of how.

Reuse or recycle batteries

From remote controls to toys to torches, many devices rely on batteries. It's important to make the most of batteries and dispose of them properly to save energy and avoid pollution.

To help with this in your home, talk to an adult about buying and using rechargeable batteries. These can be used again and again. You'll buy fewer batteries and won't need to throw as many away.

When batteries do run out, recycle them. Different local councils have different rules about recycling batteries, so make sure you check what you can recycle where.

Repair or repurpose a broken object

If you break or damage something you treasure – like a mug or a pair of jeans – see if you can fix it instead of throwing it away.

If something really can't be repaired, consider ways you might repurpose it instead of sending it to landfill.

For example:

- ☑ a mug or vase with a crack in it could be used to hold pens or paintbrushes
- ☑ a picture frame with missing glass could be turned into a jewellery holder
- ☑ if you string a few pieces of wire from one side to the other
- ☑ denim could be used to make a pencil case.

"Kintsugi" is the art of making repairs beautiful by drawing attention to them.

What could you make into something new?

Reduce food waste

Keeping the "five Rs" in mind—refuse, reduce, reuse, repurpose, and recycle—can really transform how we think about waste.

Here are a few R-based activities you could enjoy:

• give guests any packaged food, like bags of crisps or sweets, to take home with them instead of throwing it away

• pack leftover portions into reusable containers, choosing to eat them the following day or freeze them for a later date

• get creative in the kitchen: with an adult, cook up some new recipes with leftover ingredients. For example, leftovers from a roast dinner could become a chicken curry, bubble and squeak or a warm salad.

Refuse too many gifts

People give and receive gifts throughout the year – on birthdays, at new year and as little tokens of love.

This year, consider suggesting "experience gifts" rather than objects that could be broken or thrown away. These could include things like restaurant gift cards, cinema or theatre tickets, or a pass for a local museum.

These types of gifts are often better for the environment because they don't involve the production and transportation of more stuff, which uses up natural resources and can cause pollution.

Experience gifts are also fun – and the perfect way to make memories with the people you love.

Make memories at the cinema, restaurants and museums instead of collecting things.

PEOPLE POWER

DEMANDING CHANGE
Protests have been held for centuries by people wanting change, but the number has tripled in the last 15 years.

THE GREATEST THREAT TO OUR PLANET IS THE BELIEF THAT someone e
NEMO'S MUM DIDN'T DIE FOR THIS
OUR FUTURE IS IN YOUR HANDS
WE'RE LEARNING FOR A FUTURE WE DON'T HAVE
I WANT OUR EARTH TO LIVE!
WHY WOULD WE GO TO SCHOOL WHEN YOU DON'T LISTEN TO THE EDUCATED
SAVE THE ANIMALS AND OCEANS
SCOMO BRO
CH OUT SCOTT SEAT IN AMENT
NEW ENERGY NOW
DENIAL
WHAT SORT of WORLD ARE YOU LEAVING FOR US?
it's getting hot in here, so take off all your coals
#STOP ADANI LET'S MOVE AUSTRALIA BEYOND COAL
I BET DINOSA THOUGHT T AD TIME TO
YOU'RE URNING OUR UTURE
THIS ISN'T YOUR FUTURE IT'S YOUR CHILDREN'S
THIS ISN'T FINE
OUR POLITICIANS DON'T EVEN HAVE ENOUGH CENTS TO MAKE CHANGE
GIVE UP BACK OUR
future NOT
ONE WORLD ONE

EMERGING EQUALITY

More and more widely, people are putting their power into practice to increase equal opportunities and improve **accessibility** for all. There's a long way to go, but every advance matters.

Political representation

In January 2024, Mar Galcerán became Spain's first senior politician with **Down's syndrome**. As a government worker for more than 20 years, Galcerán helped change laws to benefit others with the condition. She says she wants people to be seen for their abilities, not their disabilities.

Indigenous speech makes history

In May 2024, politician Sol Mamakwa spoke to the lawmaking assembly in Ontario, Canada, in his **indigenous** language, Anishininiimowin. This was spoken widely in the region before European settlers arrived and took over.

Previously, lawmakers were allowed to speak only English or French at the assembly.

Sign language gains official status

In August 2023, South Africa's government decided that sign language would be recognised as one of the country's 12 official languages.

Campaigners had been working for nearly 30 years for the language of South Africa's four million deaf or hard-of-hearing people to be officially recognised. This makes it easier for deaf people to do well in school, go to university and apply for jobs.

Pee protests pay off

After a nine-year battle by equality protesters, more toilets for women and people who use wheelchairs are being built in Amsterdam, in the Netherlands.

Geerte Piening started the campaign after noticing far fewer loos for women than men. Now the city will invest £3.4 million in women's and wheelchair-friendly public toilets.

An accessible public toilet

TOILET DAY

World toilet day is held on 19th November each year and raises awareness of the estimated 3.5 billion people who don't have safe access to the loo.

IMPORTANT
INCLUSIVITY

Deaf dancers perform

It is often difficult for people with disabilities to take part in **cultural** or artistic activities. However, a deaf dance troupe performed in a show in Ibadan, Nigeria, aiming to challenge people's views. The dance group wanted to show the audience that people can dance without hearing the music. Troupe member Omowunmi Otunuyi said, "I'm a born dancer." In the UK, actress Rose Ayling-Ellis became the first deaf contestant on the TV show *Strictly Come Dancing*.

One of her performances was remarkable for a 15-second section danced in complete silence, giving audiences a glimpse into Ayling-Ellis's experience. It won the 2021 *Heat Unmissables Award for TV Moment of the Year* and the *British Academy Television Award for Virgin TV's Must-See Moment* in 2022, highlighting the powerful impact of her performance.

Rose Ayling-Ellis (left) with a fellow Strictly contestant

More statues for women

Denmark's culture **minister**, Jakob Engel-Schmidt, announced plans to spend up to £5.7 million putting up more statues of women. At the time, only 31 of the 321 statues in Denmark's cities were of women.

Engel-Schmidt said, "We all need role models that we can look up to."

A statue in Copenhagen of writer Lise Nørgaard

BIG BOOK
Braille takes up more space than the standard alphabet. In Braille, *Harry Potter and the Goblet of Fire* is ten volumes long.

Opera for all

An **opera** house in Milan, Italy, made its shows more accessible for people with loss of sight or hearing. La Scala released videos using subtitles, voiceovers and **sign language** about their latest performance, and provided earpieces that described the plot before each scene.

Blind opera fans in New Zealand were the first in the world to enjoy performances described by special **Braille** messages. Previously, the information was played to blind people through an earpiece, but that method often stopped. them enjoying the music.

La Scala

DAREDEVILS

Humans can impress in hundreds of thousands of ways. Some of the most attention-grabbing actions are daredevil stunts like these.

Athletes take to the skies

Eight athletes took part in a daring new sport called the Jet Suit Race Series. They each strapped a jetpack on their back and small jet engines on each arm to travel at almost 140 kilometres per hour.

The contestants raced around a one-kilometre course at a harbour in Dubai, UAE, flying between inflatable objects. It's hoped the race will get people thinking about the possibilities of jetpack technology.

A ladder to space

A ladder with 120 steps that looks as if it's floating in space opened in Loen, a small village in Norway. It was installed 790 metres above a **fjord**.

People could climb the ladder as part of a hiking route up Loen's Mount Hoven. Per Helge Bø, who created it, warned that "it might make most people's legs tremble a bit".

A head for heights gets a trim

Samuel Volery loves the mountains and hates going to the hairdressers. To combine the two, he asked his friend Julia Schuy to cut his hair while he hung upside down from a rope strung over the Swiss Alps.

Volery explained that he wanted to go out into nature and have an adventure instead of spending a boring hour at the hairdressers. He said, "I admit that the haircut was less than good, but at the same time it was free."

Samuel Volery on a mountain high-wire

FANTASTIC FINDS

Unexpected discoveries by ordinary people can reveal a lot about people's pasts and give a peek into history.

A very special type of bookmark

A woman who bought an old book found a message revealing a royal connection. Between the pages was a thank-you letter from Elizabeth Duchess of York, who became Queen Elizabeth II's mother.

The letter was more than 100 years old and was addressed to Mrs Carmichael of Dundee, Scotland. In the note, the royal writer said she had "more letters to answer than I know how to manage", but doesn't mention what the thanks are for.

When the letter went on sale in an auction, it sold for £600.

Elizabeth in the 1920s

Shipwreck spotted

Locals were astonished to come across a mysterious shipwreck that suddenly appeared on the shores of Cape Ray, Canada. Experts think stormy seas could have moved the wreck, explaining its sudden appearance.

The materials that made up the 24-metre-long wreckage suggest it could be from the 1800s. Historians hope the surviving features could teach them more about 19th-century life at sea.

Ships in a Newfoundland harbour, 1860

A drive down memory lane

94-year-old Malcolm Stern made an amazing find while trying to create a model of the car his father once owned, a yellow 1930 Talbot Darracq. While searching for reference photos, Stern found his dad's original car on an auction website.

He said the vehicle looked like a "wreck", but he bought it and spent about 1,000 hours restoring it. "I think my father would be very proud," said Stern.

A Talbot Darracq

ANCIENT FOODIE FINDS

Some specialists' discoveries reveal fascinating details about life in ancient times – including everyday diets.

Oldest bread found

The oldest known piece of modern-style bread was discovered in an ancient site called Çatalhöyük in Turkey: one of the biggest and best-preserved remains of an 8,600-year-old community.

Experts had previously found ancient "flatbread" from before that, but there is no older evidence of the modern mixing process that makes bread rise. This ancient bread had air bubbles trapped inside, along with evidence of grains.

The ruins of Çatalhöyük

A sumptuous stew

Around 80 snack stands, like today's fast-food shacks, have been discovered as **archaeologists** uncover the city of Pompeii, Italy. At one of them, experts found the remains of what the stand was serving. They discovered ancient snail shells and sheep bones, and think the stand served snail and mutton stew.

Stew pots are visible under this street-food counter.

Uncovering Pompeii

Pompeii was a thriving Roman city until a volcanic **eruption** buried it. The layers of ash and rock protected many of Pompeii's treasures from damage. Teams of archaeologists are gradually uncovering its mysteries.

Glass treasures from Pompeii

Real OR rubbish?

A cracking Roman discovery

Researchers have discovered how Romans in Britain liked their eggs in the morning.

Archaeologists found a 1,700-year-old chicken's egg in a basket. A scan showed it was hard-boiled and ready to be opened. This has led historians to believe that Romans, like modern people, had boiled eggs for breakfast.

Is this real, or a hard-boiled lie?*

*Rubbish! The egg was raw, not hard-boiled. It's the only completely preserved Roman-era egg discovered, but it reveals nothing about breakfasts.

SENSATIONAL SCIENCE

AMAZING AI

Artificial intelligence (AI) is technology that helps computers to think and create in a way similar to humans. These are some of the wonderful ways AI has been put to use.

Computer can "read" minds

A new technology creates text by scanning people's brains, potentially helping people who are unable to speak.

For the study, people had their brain activity **monitored** while they listened to podcasts. AI matched specific brain activity with certain words, and then used the matches to create text.

The results weren't always perfect, though. For example, AI translated "I don't have my driver's licence yet" to "She has not even started to learn to drive yet".

Robot writer revealed

An author who won Japan's most important writing prize revealed that she used AI to help her write her novel. Rie Kudan said around 5% of her book, Tokyo-to Dojo-to, was written by AI.

Many reactions were negative, but others think the collaboration was fitting. Kudan's novel discusses the way AI fits into life and features conversations with AI. The author said she aims to use AI as a creative tool to enhance her storytelling.

AI saves turtles from the cooking pot

A Chilean company that makes **plant-based** food used AI to make a version of turtle soup – a popular local dish – that doesn't contain turtle.

The AI studied 30,000 plants until it found five with chemicals that would taste most like turtle when mixed. The dish was created to raise awareness of turtles being endangered.

REMARKABLE ROBOTS

AI and robotics aren't the same: not all robots are intelligent, some are just programmed to carry out tasks. The marvellous mechanics can be just as impressive, though.

Robot police dog on patrol

A robot police dog was taken on a trial patrol through Malaga, Spain. The robot is designed to support police work and detect when traffic rules have been broken – for example, when electric scooters are ridden in areas where they're banned.

The robot is remote-controlled for now, but will eventually work on its own using AI.

Maintenance machine

West Japan Railway introduced a new employee to help with **maintenance**: a robot. The robot could be attached to a truck, and was able to carry up to 40 kilograms, hold a brush and use a chainsaw. Operators used it to trim tree branches along train lines and paint the frames that hold up the train cables.

A robot that moves like a mouse

Animals' bendy spines help them to move quickly and easily – something robots have found difficult. However, scientists have now invented a mouse-like robot with a flexible spine, helping it to wriggle, squeeze and turn corners. The spine allows the mouse to move 17% faster than when its spine was rigid.

Bendy spines could one day help robots take part in search-and-rescue missions, allowing them to wriggle into tight spaces where humans can't go.

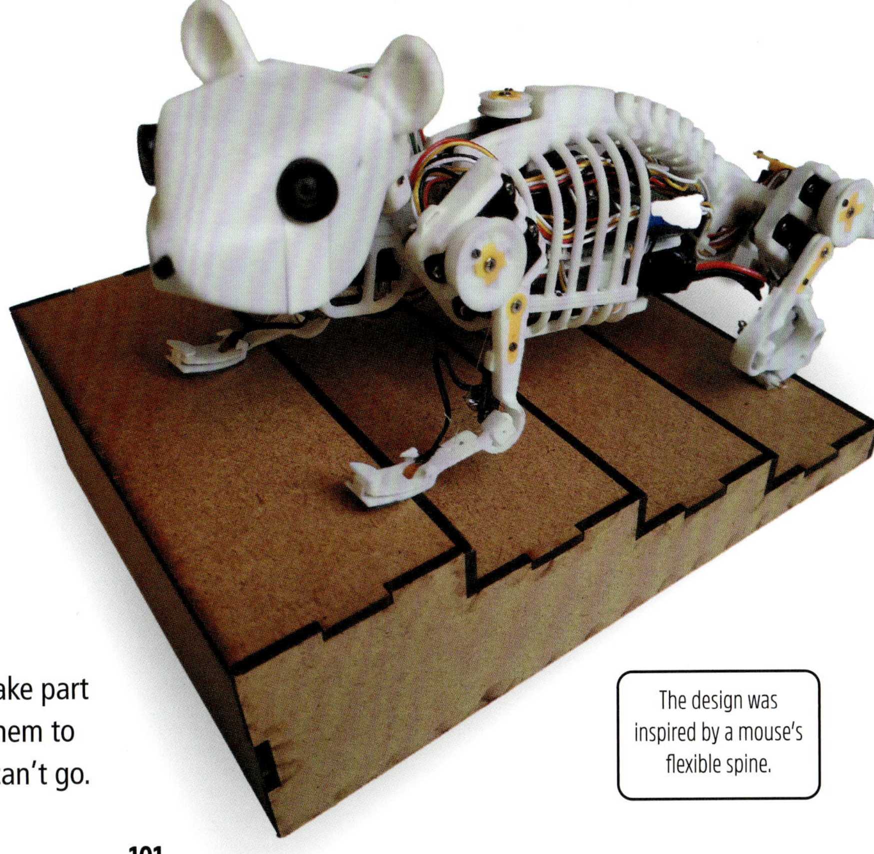

The design was inspired by a mouse's flexible spine.

INCREDIBLE INVENTIONS

Scientists are always striving to invent new devices that help people live their lives – staying healthy, getting around and doing what they love.

A people-powered water purifier

Researchers at Yonsei University, South Korea, created a water purifier powered by walking rather than batteries.

The system has a device that picks up **static electricity** from the holder's hand. The purifier can charge in 10 minutes and kills harmful bacteria and viruses. It could help people living without access to clean water and power supplies, or in places regularly hit by **natural disasters**.

Dirty water could be made safe to drink.

Feel the noise

The company Cute Circuit has developed shirts that use vibrations to help deaf football fans feel the atmosphere of a game.

In a public trial, microphones around Newcastle United's stadium captured the crowd's noise. A computer sent the information to electronic circuits in the shirts, causing tiny motors to vibrate – communicating the atmosphere of the crowd.

This initiative was such a success that the shirts will be available for games at the stadium from now on. Similar shirts have also been used to help people connect to opera performances and video games.

Could cars really fly?

Hebei Jianxin Flying Car Technology Company, based in China, bought the rights to make flying cars.

The AirCar, first developed in Europe, has a petrol engine and folding wings. It takes 2.25 minutes to transform from a car into an aircraft. In 2021, it flew for 35 minutes between two airports, reaching speeds of more than 160 kilometres per hour.

Hebei Jianxin has built its own flight school to teach driver-pilots.

An early version of the car

MEDICAL
MARVELS

Amazing inventions can also save people's lives, and help them thrive after being injured or unwell.

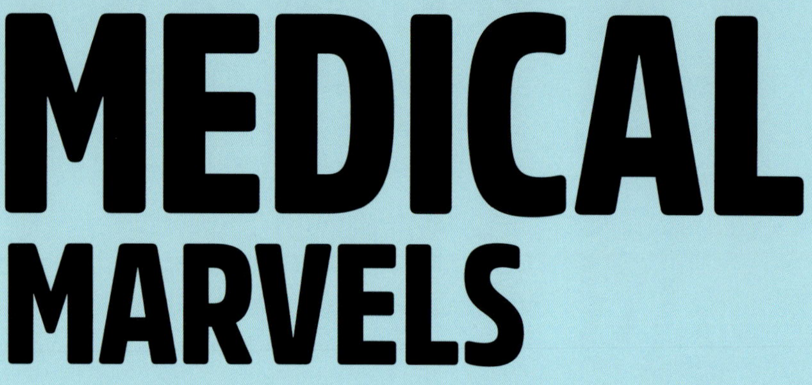

A doctor drone

A new drone can head out to deliver emergency medical supplies within 15 seconds of being called. The Everdrone E2 travels at 82 kilometres per hour, which is faster than an ambulance on the ground, and can cover a distance of eight kilometres.

The E2 carries items like EpiPens (which stop allergic reactions) and defibrillators (which use electricity to help hearts to beats regularly). It's also able to make video calls to doctors, who can instruct people who are with the patient.

Heat-sensitive prosthetic hands

S cientists have created a way for **prosthetic** hands to detect different temperatures. The MiniTouch can be used over existing prosthetics, and aims to give people who have lost limbs the sensations they've been missing.

The technology detects temperatures, and feeds this back to where the prosthetic was attached. It can sense both hot and cold, and people wearing it can even feel the warmth of another person's hand.

Regular prosthetics can't detect changes in temperature.

Device helps man to walk

A n electrical implant has dramatically improved a French man's ability to walk. Marc Gauthier has **Parkinson's disease**, and fell over several times a day until doctors put a new type of implant on his lower spine.

The device does not directly control the movement in his legs – Gauthier's brain still does that. Instead, it uses electricity to activate **nerves**, getting them to send signals telling the leg muscles to move.

It makes the whole process smoother, and now Gauthier can walk for miles.

ANTISOCIAL MEDIA?

Social media has lots of benefits: it can keep us in touch, informed and entertained. Some adults are worried about its influence on young people, though, leading to the development of controls worldwide.

Ban for under-14s

Ron DeSantis, the state governor of Florida, US, approved a law banning people under the age of 14 from joining social media. Companies would have to delete any accounts set up by anyone in Florida under 14 or risk having to pay a fine. The new rules were due to start in January 2025, but right now is the subject of many legal debates. Different groups are arguing about whether the law is fair and how it could actually work.

A smartphone that reduces distractions

A simple smartphone has been designed to reduce distractions. The Minimal Phone resembles an e-reader and can be used for calls, texts, emails and basic apps such as maps.

Minimal's features include a traditional keyboard for easy typing and a large touchscreen. The phone also has only a black-and-white display, which is good for reading but not social media use.

New screen-time ideas

France's president, Emmanuel Macron, requested a report on children's screen use. The resulting report has suggested they should not be allowed to use smartphones that have internet access until they turn 13.

It also recommended that children be banned from using social media sites until they turn 18.

These suggestions about smartphones are still being discussed in France, but haven't become official rules yet. While some schools and parents are taking the recommendations seriously, they remain guidelines rather than official legal restrictions at this point.

SPACE:
STRANGER THAN SCIENCE FICTION

Some experts think the future of the human race lies in space. Could these ideas help us make the move?

NASA plans a railway on the Moon

NASA is working to build a floating robot railway in space.

The Flexible Levitation on a Track (FLOAT) project would use magnets to float robotic trays on tracks across the surface of the Moon. Each tray could carry 30 kilograms of cargo, and the magnetised tracks could be rolled out with no damage to the Moon's surface.

Scientists at NASA hope the railway will help with its "Moon to Mars" plan.

Moon to Mars

Scientists have suggested that, far in the future, Mars may be able to support human life. NASA's "Moon to Mars" plan involves plans to build a permanent base on the Moon, from which future missions to Mars will launch.

Moon bricks made from meteorites

Carrying building materials to the Moon is expensive, but they'd be necessary for building a Moon base. Some space dust and inspiration from LEGO® might just work.

The Moon is covered in a layer of dust, but very little has been brought back to Earth. To explore how it might behave, a team ground up parts of a meteorite and mixed the dust with other materials. They used their mixture and 3D printing to create bricks that look like LEGO®.

The finished bricks are very small and won't be used on the Moon, but making them shows Moon dust could perhaps be used for building.

IDEAS FOR
SPACE

A MARS REHEARSAL

For 378 days, four volunteers lived in an artificial space base designed to imitate life on Mars. The crew grew their own vegetables and wore spacesuits to go outside for "Marswalks".

Growing fresh food in space

Until now, most space food has been pre-made like ready meals and sealed up in pouches. However, scientists are exploring ways for astronauts to grow fresh food in space, so they can replace their food stocks and have a healthier diet.

Farmbot food growers

A team at Australia's University of Melbourne is using robots to grow food, hoping to make the plant-growing process automatic. These "farmbots" can plant seeds, keep the plants watered as they grow and pick them when they're ready to eat.

The farmbots also have "E-noses", which can detect the smells given off by the plants. Used with sensors in the soil, the technology can work out what the plants need.

A farmbot

New hints of ancient water on Mars

A Chinese **rover** on Mars has found patterns in rocks beneath the planet's surface that suggest water may have been present.

The rover took measurements using a special instrument that examines what lies below the planet's surface. The shapes of the rocks they scanned resemble patterns formed on Earth when water freezes and melts, so may be a clue in the search for Mars's lost water.

BRILLIANT
BOOKS

CELEBRATING
BOOKS
World Book Day is held in the UK
every year, on the first Thursday in
March. People all over the country
celebrate books, enjoy book-themed
activities and dress up as their
favourite characters.

AUTHORS LOVE THEIR LIBRARIES

Libraries are some of the most magical places on Earth. They provide a wealth of knowledge, offer an escape into other worlds and create opportunities for everyone. They've also inspired thousands of writers.

Grab a book!

Libraries are magical worlds of imagination for Joseph Coelho, the UK Children's Laureate. Growing up near a local library, he discovered amazing books about mysterious creatures and fell in love with reading. Now a successful writer, Coelho believes libraries are incredible community spaces where kids can explore stories, join fun clubs, and find inspiration. He even visited 213 libraries across the UK to celebrate these special places that help children discover the joy of reading and writing.

A tour to celebrate libraries

One in seven primary schools in the UK doesn't have a library, so The National Literacy Trust ran a campaign to persuade the government to provide money to help.

As part of the campaign, Jeff Kinney, the author of the *Diary of a Wimpy Kid* series, toured the UK celebrating the power of reading. He hosted contests that could award books or money to local libraries.

Kinney is grateful that he had a school library. "I think that reading just enhances your life," he explained. "It makes you more interesting as a person. It helps you to step into somebody else's mind."

At the same time, he believes that reading helps people to explore their own minds. "I think it's really important for a kid to see their own experience reflected back to them in the pages of a book," Kinney said.

FUN FEATURES
IN LIBRARIES

Bookshelves and reading corners are brilliant, but they're not the only reasons for book-lovers to visit libraries. Check out the surprising things for which these libraries are famous.

Bats

At the 300-year-old Joanina Library in the University of Coimbra, Portugal, an unlikely species of librarian protects the books. Every night, bats emerge from the enormous bookcases and eat insects that can destroy old paper and glue.

Karaoke corner

The Tikkurila Library in Vantaa, Finland, has a soundproof **karaoke room**, with thousands of songs on offer. It must be seen as the ultimate study break!

Real OR rubbish?

A cat gallery

Instead of having to pay for lost or damaged books, people could turn up to a library in Massachusetts, US, with their best cat drawings, paintings or photographs. People who brought in pictures could choose to have them added to the gallery.

Is this true – or have we told an appawlling lie?*

*Real! The gallery was only temporary, but it did exist. It was part of an event called "March Meowness"; a month of cat-themed activities.

A dividing line

The Haskell Free Library features a line that separates Quebec in Canada from Vermont in the US. Standing across the line means visitors can read a book in two countries at once.

The feel of a forest

Beijing City Library, China features giant fake trees with "leaves" that form the roof of the building. At the centre, a walkway resembles the bottom of a valley with twists and turns that copy the path of Beijing's Tonghui River.

READY TO READ?

Books are more than words on a page. A book can give you new skills, take you to new places and transform you into different people as you read.

Top tips for ready readers

Want to make the most of your reading experience? Try these tips for enjoying your brilliant books.

- ☑ **Give yourself space and time**. Find a comfortable spot, and start by reading for up to one hour at a time so you don't run out of steam.

- ☑ **Look for connections with characters**. Seeing a character encounter similar experiences and overcome challenges can make you feel less alone.

- ☑ **Bond over your books**. Chatting about funny stories and exciting ideas will make you feel more connected to others.

- ☑ **Don't be afraid to try new things**. Try dipping into non-fiction and **poetry as well as fiction.**

- ☑ **Tie in some activities**. Keep firing up your engagement and imagination by getting involved. For example, you could draw the characters in the story or find out more about the setting.

Reading heroes

KEEP A BOOK JOURNAL

Keeping a book journal is a really useful way of reminding yourself what you've read – and can be fun and creative, too. Here are four tips to help you start out.

1. Choose your format

Decide how you'd like to keep your book journal. You could write a computer document, so you can go back and make changes. You could use a notebook, which can boost **creativity** because you can add things like drawings and doodles. You could even record entries as videos.

2. Decide on details

Adding particular details in all entries helps you to compare books. Including the titles and the authors' names is a must. You could include the dates you started and finished a book, and its **genre**. You could also add a **summary** of the book.

3. Write your review

Write what you thought of each book. Did you enjoy it? Why is that? What was the best thing about it and the worst thing about it?

To make your journal more individual, you could write out your favourite quote or list the emotions you felt reading it. Perhaps you could note down something it taught you, or some facts you don't want to forget.

4. Add your own creativity

Could you use your journal to create something new? Perhaps you could write a poem about a character, rewrite the ending or draw a picture of a scene. You could even start a new writing project by writing a book's sequel.

READY TO WRITE?

Writing isn't just an activity you do at school; it's something you can do by yourself for your own benefit. From writing messages to your friends to making plans, and from answering questions at school to talking with your family, words are amazing tools for communicating all sorts of things.

What can writing do for you?

Learning to understand your thoughts and feelings is a big part of life – and writing about them can help a lot. Research shows keeping a diary can help to improve your confidence, reduce anxiety and boost your mood. Working things out on the page can also be a great way of solving problems.

Express yourself

Sarah Ratermann Beahan is a teacher who helps people express their emotions through writing.

"Writing about feelings, situations and experiences can help manage big emotions," she explains.

"Writing the story of our experience helps to figure out what we are feeling. It's called 'naming'. When we name our experience, we can figure out what to do with it."

Don't worry about the rules

When you're writing for yourself, the focus is on what you think and feel, rather than getting things right or sounding clever.

Beahan says, "It's more important to let your story and feelings flow. This writing is for you alone and the process of putting it on paper is more important than how clear or correct it is."

- Write regularly about your day. What happened, how did you feel, what emotions came up?

- Describe something that you're proud of. What did you accomplish and why was this important to you?

- What is something you'd like to change or do differently and why? What's one step you can take towards that?

HOW TO... WRITE POETRY

Poetry can be sensitive – and it can also be silly! These kinds of short poem help to show its range.

Haikus

Haikus are a type of poem developed in Japan. They usually reflect on specific moments in time.

The rules

A haiku should be three lines long and have 17 **syllables**: five in the first and last lines, and seven in the middle line. It doesn't need to rhyme.

The inspiration

Step outside and explore the world with all your senses. Notice the small details: the way sunlight falls on leaves, the rhythm of wind through grass, the subtle changes in the air. Listen to the sounds around you - birdsong, rustling branches, distant sounds. Feel the textures of bark, stones, or grass. Let these experiences guide your writing and spark your imagination.

Experiment with sense, rhythm and flow by using words with different numbers of syllables.

Cherry blossoms bloom –
Petals falling like snowflakes
Whisper of springtime.

Limericks

Limericks are a type of short poem developed in Ireland, and usually poke fun at a character.

The rules

In limericks, lines 1, 2 and 5 rhyme together, and each has three big beats. Lines 3 and 4 are shorter, with two big beats, and rhyme with each other. (The beats are underlined in the example.)

The inspiration

- Line 1: Introduce a silly character.
- Line 2: Describe something odd they did.
- Lines 3 and 4: Give more details.
- Line 5: Describe the result – the sillier the better!

A <u>cur</u>ious <u>wom</u>an named <u>Sue</u>
Made <u>sand</u>wiches <u>filled</u> with <u>glue</u>.
Her <u>lips</u> made a <u>smack</u>,
And they <u>stuck</u>, front and <u>back</u>,
She now <u>hums</u> to <u>speak</u> – it's <u>true</u>!

ASTONISHING ARTS

COOL CANVASES

Artistic images aren't just hung in galleries: they can pop up anywhere. These innovative artists have chosen unusual places to show off their skills.

Modern art at an ancient site

An outdoor **exhibition** of modern art was set up next to the ancient Pyramids of Giza in Egypt.

The exhibition, called "Forever Is Now", was designed to do no damage to the 4,500-year-old site. The pieces, created by 14 artists, sit on sand brought from elsewhere, so they don't even touch the real ground.

Farmer creates artwork in rice fields

A farmer in Chiang Rai, Thailand, worked with more than 200 volunteers to create artworks of cats in a rice field.

Tanyapong Jaikham started the project in October 2023 and used different types of rice plant to create his designs of cartoon cats. As the plants grow, their colours change over time, revealing the cat designs.

Art transforms tunnel

An underground art **installation** has opened in a 10.5 kilometre road tunnel that connects two of the Faroe Islands in the north Atlantic Ocean.

Faroese artist Edward Fuglø came up with 10 artworks, inspired by legends of the islands, to light up the tunnel walls. As drivers travel through the tunnel, they can tune in their car radios to hear a piece of music specially created to go with the art.

Land artist inspired by nature

An artist in West Yorkshire, UK, creates outdoor masterpieces using natural objects he finds.

Winston Plowes says his "land art" patterns can take up to nine hours to complete. The stones, sticks, leaves and berries he uses then naturally fade back into the beaches, fields or forests.

Plowes says, "Working on a beach, it's like having a giant Etch-A-Sketch — twice a day, the whole thing is going to be wiped clean."

He keeps a record of his artworks by photographing them, and encourages everyone to have a go.

"Art is for everybody," he says.

Land art can be created by anyone, anywhere.

EXTRAORDINARY EXHIBITIONS

Even in galleries, art can be surprising – and these exhibitions are undoubtedly unexpected.

Art turns its back to visitors

Visitors to the Prado in Madrid, Spain, saw a new side to the museum's artwork.

An exhibition called "Reversos" (Spanish for "on the reverse"), showed what paintings look like from behind. Curators said it explored the secrets hidden behind the art.

Museum exhibits fake art

The Vancouver Art Gallery in Canada received unfinished paintings supposedly made by famous artist J.E.H. MacDonald – but, after a long investigation, realised the artworks were fakes.

Nevertheless, curators had become so fond of the **forgeries** they decided to display them anyway. "These works are inspiring in their own right," one curator said.

Is this story a fake, or are we painting it in its true colours?*

*__Rubbish!__ The museum did display the forged artworks, but it was in an exhibition about the investigation that revealed they were fakes, allowing visitors to peek behind the scenes at the work curators do.

Artist's cunning plan backfires

A budding artist got into trouble after he hung up his own artwork at a gallery in Germany. The artist, who worked at the gallery, sneaked in early one morning to drill two holes in the wall and put up his painting. He had hoped the public would recognise his talent, but unfortunately other staff members noticed the painting immediately. The man was promptly sacked and banned from the gallery.

MINI MASTERPIECES

These artworks may be little, but they show their artists' big talent.

Micro Stonehenge sits on a pin

A British "micro artist" created the world's smallest Stonehenge sculpture: it was so tiny that it fitted on the head of a pin.

The miniature model was created using a **microscope**, and each stone measured between 0.1 millimetres and 0.7 millimetres – the thickness of one human hair. It took artist David A. Lindon three months to make.

"A single twitch from my fingers can wreck months of work," he said. The artist has also created micro versions of popular paintings such as Van Gogh's *The Starry Night*.

The teeny house fit for a queen

Queen Mary, wife of George V (British king between 1910–1936), is proof that we are never too old or too grand for toys. She owned the world's largest dolls' house, which a cousin gave her more than 100 years ago.

The grand little house is currently on display at Windsor Castle, UK. It has electricity, running water and working lifts. There's a grand piano, delicate furniture, a library of tiny novels by famous authors and even a mini version of the UK **Crown Jewels**, with real gems.

A tastefully teeny-tiny artwork

Food company Birds Eye asked an artist to create the world's smallest fish-finger sandwich, complete with lettuce and a delicate dollop of ketchup.

Crafted in clay by artist Nadia Michaux, the mini meal took more than 100 hours to make. It was a centimetre tall and weighed about the same as a pea.

The process was demanding, Michaux said. "This was a difficult challenge, given that the size of this sandwich makes up no more than four 5p coins stacked on top of each other, and each fish finger measures around five millimetres by 11 millimetres."

Birds Eye had first asked the public what makes the perfect fish-finger sandwich. It was butter, white bread, ketchup and lettuce.

Working wool into little wonders

A Japanese artist called Terumi Ohta spends hundreds of hours creating miniature sculptures of people's pets.

Ohta uses a technique called "needle felting" to form different types of wool into shapes. She has spent 15 years mastering the craft and says her goal is to make the most life-like creations she can.

The artist says she pays extremely close attention to every detail of an animal so that it's instantly recognisable. Her most difficult creation was a short-haired miniature pinscher dog, which took her more than 500 hours.

FANTASTIC FASHION

Iris Apfel, fashion designer

Some artists use fashion design to display their ideas in kooky clothes. Would you wear any of these?

Wrapped in luxury

A woman from Liverpool, UK, has set up a business designing dresses made from old tea towels.

Scarlett Hawkes started sewing when she was 14 and loved upcycling clothes from her mum. Her first big success was when she turned a Heinz ketchup tea towel into a dress.

"People absolutely loved it," she said.

Hawkes has gone on to sell tea-towel dresses, jackets and skirts. Customers can even send in their own tea towels to be used.

High-fashion towel

For most people, bathroom towels are meant for drying. However, a luxury fashion company called Balenciaga had other ideas.

The knee-length towel skirt is for men and women, and has fastenings on the inside. When it's worn, it looks like someone has tied a towel around their waist – but Balenciaga put it on sale for £695.

A fuzzy fashion show

At Paris Fashion Week, a model dressed as a big ball of fur bumped her way down the catwalk.

The costume had eye holes, but model Mi'jon Woods could see only "shadows of things". The fuzzy ball collided with singer Sam Smith, who was performing live, before crashing into the audience.

"Came into my first Paris Fashion Week show like a wrecking ball," Woods joked on social media.

Real OR rubbish?

Woolly jumpers made from hair

Have you ever wondered what happens to the hair that hairdressers chop off? Although it's mostly thrown away, one company has found a use for it.

Human Material Loop spins human hair waste to create fabric for clothing. Its first products included a jumper, a blazer and an outdoor coat padded with the hair.

Is this story real, or is it a hair-larious lie?*

*Rubbish! The company hopes other designers will buy its fabric to use in their own designs too.

DRAMATIC DANCE

For some, there's art in movement. What do you think people can communicate through dance?

Moving for your mood

Dance has definite positive effects on mood, experts say. Dance can express things without a language barrier, making connections. Getting lost in music can take our minds off worries. Dancing is also a workout, which releases feel-good chemicals in our brains.

22-year-old dancer Virginie Magumba, who won Best Congolese Dancer in Goma, Democratic Republic of the Congo, said, "Dancing helps me liberate myself, manage my emotions and not feel all alone."

Passinho

Passinho is a dance style created by young people in the poorest areas of Rio de Janeiro, Brazil. It combines different dancing styles such as breakdancing and samba. In 2024, passinho was given "cultural heritage status", meaning it is officially recognised as an important art form.

Real OR rubbish?

Minister orders: stop the bop

Many vehicles in Cambodia are fitted with horns that play tunes instead of making the usual "honk". These have become so popular that videos shared on social media show people bopping along to them beside the road.

However, the Cambodian prime minister decided the dancing was "inappropriate" and dangerous. As a result, he banned all musical horns. Is this real, or are we playing the wrong note?*

* **Real!** Dancing to horns in public places was outlawed – but who knows about private parties? "Good," says the man, "because it's his birthday."

MARVELLOUS MUSIC

Music can be moving and emotional – but it can also be just plain odd!

Whistling through her nose

LuLu Lotus discovered as a child that she had a natural talent for nose whistling, which is when someone makes musical sounds by controlling the way air flows out of their nose.

After years of practice, she qualified for a **Guinness World Record**: the volume of her nose whistle was measured at 44.1 decibels – about as loud as a bird call.

Long song carries on

An **organ** in Halberstadt, Germany, has been playing the same piece of music since 2001. In February 2024, it played new notes for the first time since February 2022. The organ should now play the same sound until 5 August 2026.

The piece, called *As Slow as Possible*, was created by John Cage. It isn't due to end until the year 2640.

Rapping across the ages

A group of women in their 80s gained popularity for their music about farm life. Their hip-hop group, Suni and the Seven Princesses, first performed at a community centre in 2023. They were watched by only a few local people at the time, but achieved nearly 80,000 views on YouTube.

Cork kids set music world on fire

A rap song by a group of children gained more than 8.6 million views. *The Spark* was written by members of the Kabin Studio, a youth arts centre in Cork, Ireland, and **refugee** children living in Ireland. The song became an anthem for Cruinniú na nÓg, a festival celebrating young people's creativity.

EAT FOR CHANGE
Eating plant-based food can help to save the world: people who eat no meat create 75% fewer emissions than major meat eaters.

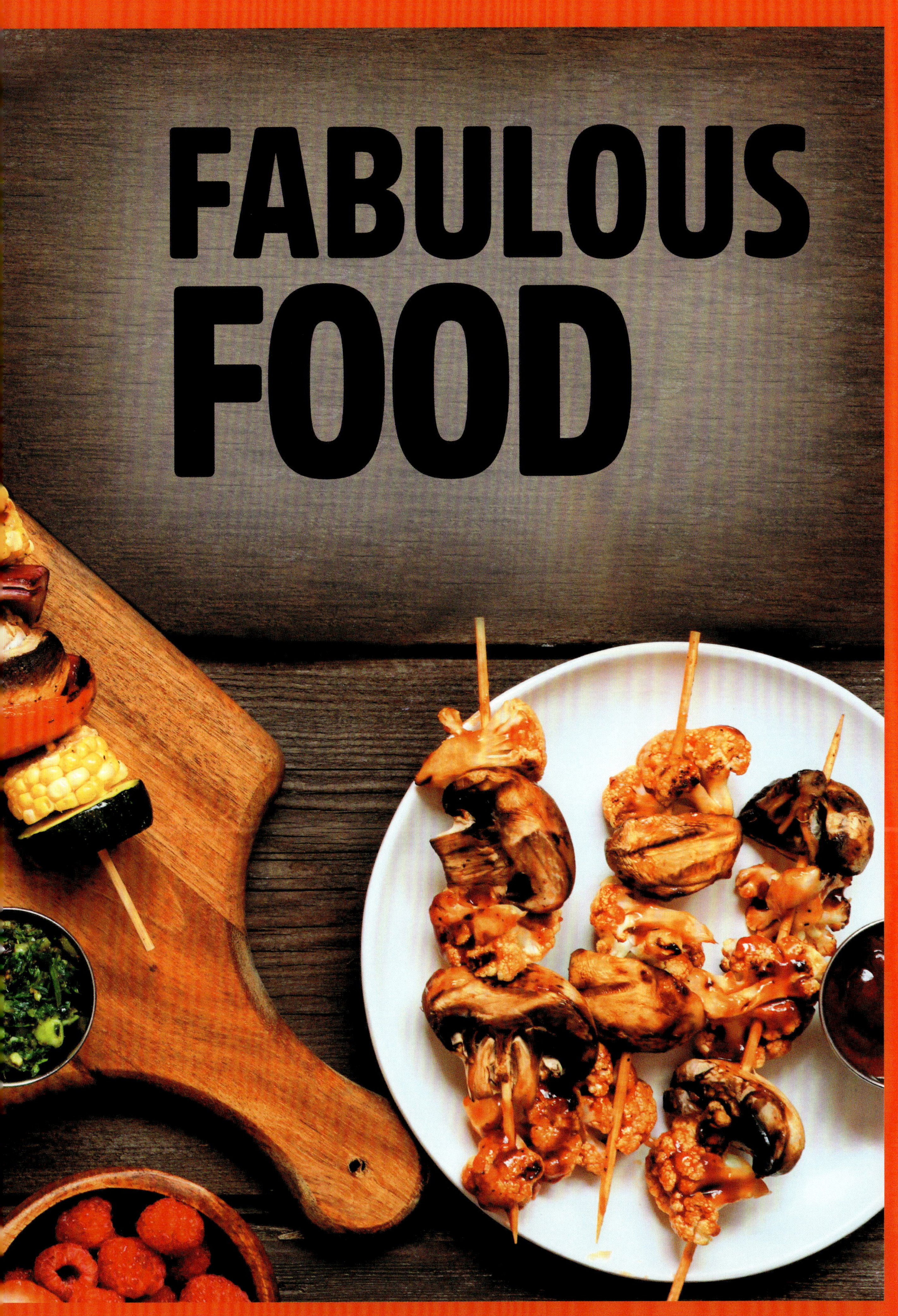

FABULOUS
FOOD

GROCERIES ... OR JUST GROSS?

Strange tastes can split opinions – even if there's good reasoning behind them. Do any of these ideas get your taste-buds tingling?

A fishy food source

A Finland-based company has created a bone paste that can be added to meat. SuperGround grinds fish or chicken bones, briefly heats them to high temperatures and then grinds them again to form a paste.

When added to food, the paste provides extra nutrients. It can be mixed with meat products so they can feed more people, which is better for the environment.

Bugs are on the menu

The Singapore Food Agency (SFA) has approved 16 insects as safe for humans to eat. The list includes crickets, grasshoppers, mealworms, moths and a particular species of honeybee.

Eating insects is an environmentally friendly way to add protein to your diet. Farming them doesn't use as much space or water as raising **livestock** such as cows.

SNACK TIME
Insect snacks include choco-fruit mealworms, cricket cookies and tangy ants for seasoning.

How many salts in your tea?

Relations between UK and US tea-lovers recently became strained after a US scientist claimed that the perfect cup of tea needs a pinch of salt.

Michelle Francl came to her **theory** after looking at texts that were more than 1,000 years old. Her claim caused some strong reactions, though, and US representatives in the UK had to step in.

In a post on social media on 24th January 2024, the embassy said, "When it comes to tea, we stand as one."

CRAZY FOR CRISPS

Many say the salty crunch of crisps is the perfect savoury snack – for some, opening a bag is an obsession.

Haggis here to stay

Grace, a 10-year-old girl from Edinburgh, Scotland, received a year's supply of her favourite crisps – haggis and black pepper – after she wrote to the crisp company. Taylors Snacks had planned to sell its haggis crisps only in winter, but Grace asked for the flavour to remain on the shelves all year.

"If you can, thanks," she wrote, "if not I will be sad."

Haggis crisps are now back on shops' shelves.

1970s crisp packet unearthed

Plastic takes a long time to break down.

Aman in Poole, UK, dug up a surprisingly intact 49-year-old crisp packet in his garden.

Cenk Albayrak-Touye was gardening when he discovered the old Quavers packet. It showed the date 31 October 1975, which was while Quavers ran a contest to win the board game "Sporting SuperSix".

Albayrak-Touye said, "It's like a little time capsule."

Collector decides to "pack-et" in

Gary Key had an unusual collection: more than 24,000 crisp packets, collected over 12 years. He was so well known for his collection that everyone he knew saved empty packets for him.

Now, however, he's stopped collecting. Instead, he decided to make small garden fountains from the packets, to raise money for charity.

PERFECT PLATEFULS

Who decides what makes a perfect meal? Scientists, lawmakers and chefs have all tried.

It's crunch time for scientists

UK scientists have been using the latest technology to discover what makes the perfect biscuit crunch.

Experts from the University of Warwick, UK, and chocolate company Cadbury built an oven inside an **x-ray machine**. They scanned different biscuits every 20 seconds to uncover the ideal baking time, thickness and recipe for the ultimate eating experience.

Cadbury scientist Thomas Curwen said that he hopes the study will help them to "deliver the great-tasting biscuits of the future".

Protected for perfection

A selection of foods from the UK, including Cornish pasties and Staffordshire cheese, have been given "protected **status**" in Japan. This means that certain British foods sold by companies in Japan will need to be made in the UK and sent over.

The special status is designed to stop people from making and selling copies of the food, keeping the quality high and the taste experience as intended.

Steak dinner with a grand price

Soon after opening, the UK restaurant Aragawa offered customers steaks for astonishing prices up to £900.

The expensive "Tajima" beef comes from a special type of cow from a small farm in Japan, and has to meet strict standards for colour and texture. Chef Kazuo Imayosh spent 40 years perfecting the art of cooking it. He says he can tell when a steak is ready just by touching it and listening to the sizzle.

A PIZZA
THE ACTION

People eat pizza all over the world. In fact, experts think more than 5 billion pizzas are sold worldwide every year. It's no wonder they can be headline news!

Pizza "horrors" on display

From banana in South Africa to crickets in Thailand, people top their pizzas with all sorts of weird ingredients.

At a food fair in Naples, Italy, an organisation called Coldiretti put "a gallery of horrors" on show with the most disgusting pizzas from around the world. The award for the worst pizza went to one from Hong Kong that was topped with snake.

The world's cheesiest pizza

Two French chefs took a world record for putting the most varieties of cheese on a pizza.

They chopped small cubes from a whopping 1,001 varieties and placed all of them on a sturdy pre-baked crust. They then put the gooey monstrosity back in the oven to melt.

Pizza delivery "rocketship" for sale

A rare vehicle was put up for sale in Las Vegas, US. The 1985 Tritan A2 Aerocar was actually designed to deliver pizzas.

The car can carry two passengers and is fitted with heaters to keep the pizzas warm. The previous owner made a big profit: he bought the vehicle in 2021 for about $25,000 (almost £20,000), and auctioned it off for $32,000 (nearly £25,250).

MAKE **PIZZA DIP** with **GARLIC KNOTS**

Pizza dip

Ingredients:

- 225 g cream cheese
- 100 g grated mozzarella
- 100 g grated Parmesan
- 1 teaspoon oregano
- 250 g of tomato pizza/pasta sauce
- toppings of your choice (e.g. pepperoni or mushrooms)

Instructions:

1. Preheat your oven to 220°C.
2. Mix the oregano, cream cheese, half of the mozzarella and half of the Parmesan.
3. Spread the mixture into a small baking dish.
4. Spoon the tomato sauce over the cheese mixture.
5. Top with the rest of the mozzarella and Parmesan, and any other toppings you like.
6. Bake for about 20 minutes, until the cheese is melted and bubbly.

Garlic knots

Ingredients:

- a 400 g packet of pizza dough
- 4 tablespoons butter
- 2 cloves garlic, chopped

Instructions :

1. Slice the dough into 16 strips.
2. Tie each strip in a knot.
3. Arrange the knots on baking try lined with greaseproof paper.
4. Bake for about 15 minutes, until puffed and golden.
5. While the knots bake, melt the butter on low heat. Add the garlic and stir continuously for 3 minutes.
6. When they're done, brush your dough knots with the garlic butter.

Dip your garlic knots into the dip and enjoy!

SUPER -SIZED

Some clever cooks and shocked shoppers have taken the idea of "super-sized" food to the next level.

Invasion of the mutant crisps

Ollie Skinner-Foster, aged eight, found a whopping 10-centimetre Frazzle in his crisps packet. He was so pleased that he refused to eat it, instead putting the super-sized snack on display in his bedroom.

A similar snack shock was had by Michael Langford. In his packet of cheese and onion crisps, he found a 15-centimetre "mutant" crisp nearly the full length of the packet.

After the discovery hit newspapers, Langford **auctioned** his find to raise money for charity.

A super-sized croissant to share

Lewis Gill, who owns a café in Scotland, baked croissants large enough to feed several people. The enormous pastries sold for £20 each.

Gill used 300 grams of butter for each one, and they were so big that he could fit only two in the oven at once.

"It's quite a challenge," he said. "You have 60 steps along the way where you can go wrong."

The world's biggest guacamole dip

A festival of avocados in Peribán, Mexico, set the world record for the biggest bowl of guacamole.

The dip, made from avocados, tomatoes, onions and lime, took 300 people around three hours to create. It weighed in at 4,970 kilograms.

Francisco Farías, who was at the festival, said, "For such a large guacamole, the ingredients were perfect. Everything was well balanced."

CHEESY
TALES

Cheese can be creamy, crunchy or stinky; it come from cows, sheep, goats or even plants. What's your cheesy choice?

A champion cheese

The World Cheese Awards attracts makers from all over the world – in 2024, 4,500 competitors gathered to battle for first place.

In the end, a blue cheese from Norway took the trophy. Judges commended the winner for its "creaminess" and "fruity overtones".

"This means so much to us," said Maren Gangstad, who made the cheese with her husband, Ole.

Cheese-packaging protests

Cheese traditionalists were in uproar after an environmentally friendly law was passed.

Wooden boxes that are used to package French Camembert cheese came under threat when the European Union made rules for recyclable packaging.

Although the change may seem minimal, some people in France protested that this endangered traditions. However, many Camembert cheeses have "protected" status – meaning protesters won't be cheesed off.

Mac and cheeseless

In the US, popular brand Kraft made a more environmentally friendly version of its beloved Mac & Cheese. The product is now available in a plant-based dish.

Kraft sells more than a million boxes of the classic version every day, and has used the same recipe for 85 years. The company said its "NotMac&Cheese" would still offer "the creamy and comforting experience … without the dairy".

MAKE
WELSH RAREBIT

Have all those cheesy stories got your appetite going? Have a go at making this cheese-based treat from Wales.

Ingredients

- 225 g mature cheddar cheese, grated
- 25 g butter, melted
- 1 tablespoon Worcestershire sauce
- 1 tablespoon mustard
- 1 tablespoon plain flour
- Freshly ground black pepper
- 4 tablespoons milk
- 4 thick slices of bread

Instructions

1. Put the grated cheese, butter, Worcestershire sauce, mustard, flour and a pinch of black pepper in a saucepan and mix it well.

2. Put the pan on a gentle heat and stir it until the mixture is melted.

3. Gradually add the milk until the mixture has become a thick paste. (Take care not to make it too wet.)

4. Remove the pan from the heat and leave it to cool a little.

5. Toast the bread lightly.

6. Spread the cheesy mixture on one side of each piece of toast.

7. Grill gently until the topping is cooked through, bubbling and nicely browned.

OUT AND
ABOUT

BRIGHT LIGHTS
Cities cover only 2% of the world's land, but more than half of all people live in them. Experts believe this will rise to 70% by 2050.

Up, Up and away!

Holiday rental company AIrbnb has created a replica of the house from Disney and Pixar's film "*Up*."

Located in Abiquiu, US, the house featured more than 8,000 balloons. People could apply to stay and would be emailed a "golden ticket" if successful. Airbnb advertised that guests could even watch the house "fly away" (lifted by a crane).

The hotel was part of Airbnb's "Icons" series. Guests were also able to spend the night in the Ferrari Museum in Maranello, Italy, the Musée d'Orsay in Paris, France and even the home of a film star in Chennai, India.

The fungus campsite

A project in the Czech Republic aimed to "grow" a little house from **fungus**.

The "SAMOROST" house was designed to look like two parasol mushrooms, and was put together using a material called mycelium: thin, root-like fibres from fungi. Mycelium can't carry much weight, but it was possible to shape it to fit out the walls, ceiling and furniture.

The designers hoped to offer visitors an environmentally friendly luxury camping experience rooted in nature.

Holiday inside a pancake paradise

Visitors to the Eggo House of Pancakes in Tennessee, US, could experience life inside a stack of pancakes.

The holiday-rental home was a tribute to the all-American breakfast, with a chimney shaped like a block of butter and bed sheets themed with strawberries and cream. There was a freezer full of ready-made pancakes and even a maple-syrup fountain.

TERRIBLE TOURISM

Some of the ways officials reach out to attract tourists seem simply bizarre.

A relaxing roadside?

A **council** in Stretford, UK, set up sun loungers by a busy road. The chairs allowed people to put their feet up and take in the view of passing traffic.

People pointed out that bad weather would mean they couldn't be used a lot of the time, and accused the council of wasting money. Others jokingly named the site "Stretford Beach".

Tourists invited up tower

An attraction in New York, US, invited tourists to recreate one of history's most famous photographs - the 1932 'Lunch atop a Skyscraper.' In the original, 11 construction workers sat casually on a steel beam 260 metres above Manhattan. Today's visitors can safely experience a similar thrill, strapped securely to a special beam that lifts them high above the city for their own memorable photo.

Real OR rubbish?

Inviting aliens for a visit

The tourism bureau of Lexington, US, targeted adverts at a star system with Earth-sized planets 40 light-years away. It beamed "Visit Lexington, Kentucky" into space, with a recording of blues music and photos of the city. The appeal is expected to arrive there in about 38 years.

Is this story too far-out to be true?*

*Rubbish! The leader said Lexington is "the ideal location for extraterrestrial travellers to begin." No spaceships have arrived so far, but visits to the city's website have risen by more than 50%.

WAY TO GO!

Planes, trains, cars, bikes, buses and on foot – people get around in lots of ways. Sometimes, travel tales and varied vehicles can be newsworthy.

LONGEST BIKE

A team of two had to ride their 55-metre-long creation for 100 metres to earn the record.

An incredible colour-changing car

The BMW i Vision Dee **concept** car allows drivers to change their minds easily: a special coating can transform it into 32 different colours. The car can also make facial expressions using its headlights.

Turbo teenager beats the Tube

A super-speedy teenager beat a London underground train in a "race the Tube" challenge. The craze started 10 years ago and involves getting off a train and running to the next stop to catch the same train again.

Rupert Brindley, aged 15, had just one minute and 49 seconds to race between Shepherd's Bush Market and Goldhawk Road. He took the challenge early on a Saturday morning when few people were around, to make sure he didn't bump into anyone.

Rupert, who finished with time to spare, said, "I still smile and laugh when I think about it; I can't believe I'm faster than the Circle Line!"

Avoiding the air

Torbjørn C. Pedersen, also known as Thor, completed a 10-year challenge of visiting every country in the world without flying on a plane.

He left his home in Denmark to start the challenge in 2013. He travelled to 203 countries using a mixture of boats, buses, taxis and trains before finishing his journey in the Maldives.

UNIQUE WAYS TO TRAVEL

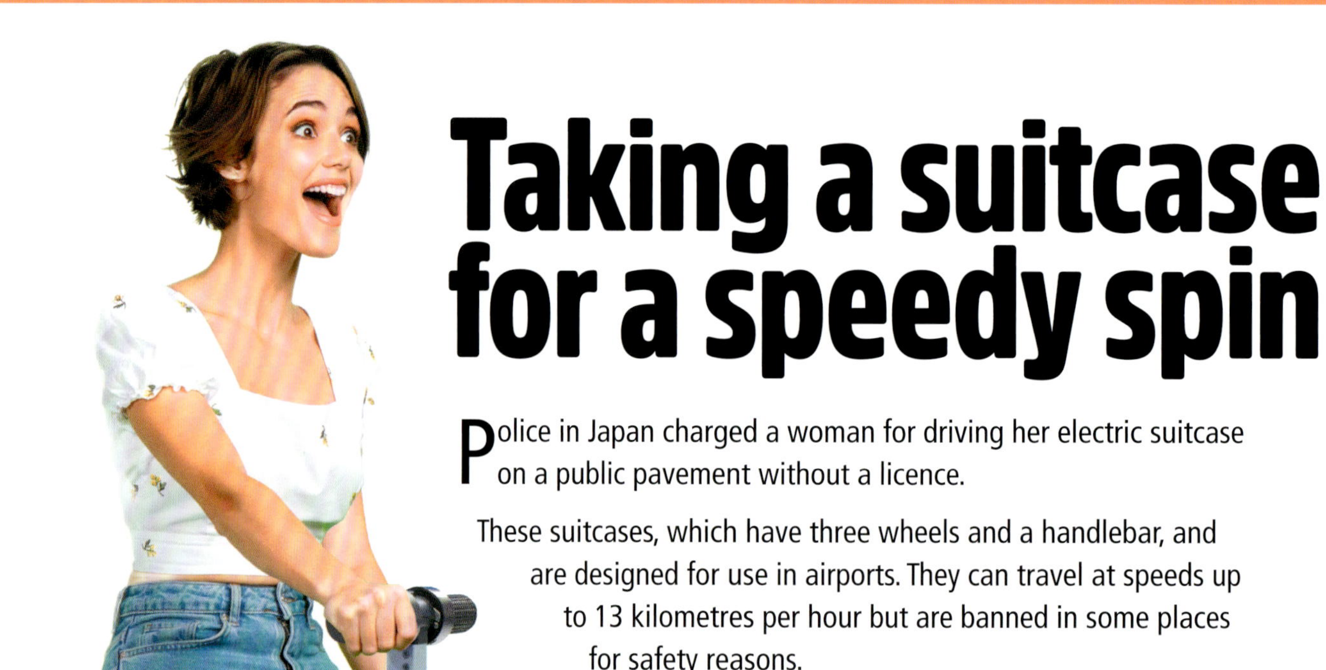

Taking a suitcase for a speedy spin

Police in Japan charged a woman for driving her electric suitcase on a public pavement without a licence.

These suitcases, which have three wheels and a handlebar, and are designed for use in airports. They can travel at speeds up to 13 kilometres per hour but are banned in some places for safety reasons.

The woman reportedly told police, "I did not think a driving licence was required."

TRAIN DELAYS

In Japan, if your train is running more than 5 minutes late you can get a special certificate to show your boss or teacher to explain why you're late.

Alex the rabbit drives to fame

A huge rabbit bunny-hopped to fame after videos of him in a miniature electric car were shared on social media. Alex, who weighed more than 13 kilograms at the time, attended charity events and calmed patients in hospitals.

The rolling rabbit was rescued by Kei Kato and Josh Row in 2020. Kei, who owns a restaurant in San Francisco, US, said, "He makes people feel better – and he loves the attention, too."

Alex the bunny

Real OR rubbish?

Only ghosts board this bus

A so-called "ghost bus" departs each week from West Ealing station, London, UK. Very few people know about the route, its timetable is not advertised and passengers cannot buy a ticket on board. The spooky bus doesn't return after arriving at its destination.

Is this story real, or are we taking you for a ride?*

*Real! The bus replaced a rarely used train service, and the train company said closing the route would be complicated and expensive. They believe the bus is great for "quirky journeys for transport enthusiasts".

ODD JOBS

People get paid for all kinds of weird and wonderful work. Do any of these jobs appeal to you?

Jokers called to brighten breakfast

A hotel in Glasgow, Scotland, was on the look-out for a comedian willing to "crack jokes and eggs" during the Edinburgh Festival Fringe, a performance festival that features lots of comedy shows.

In exchange for entertaining breakfast guests, the comedian was offered their train fares to Scotland and a place to stay. Any so-called "breakfast **banter** butlers" were invited to apply by sending a video of themselves performing a a simple breakfast-related joke.

Calling all superfans

The Victoria and Albert Museum in London, UK, houses more than 2.8 million objects that cover 5,000 years of human creativity. However, it felt its staff were lacking in a few important areas of pop culture.

The museum advertised for "superfan" advisers to help. They were asked to teach the staff about some surprising special subjects for possible future exhibitions, including superstar Taylor Swift, emojis and the shoe brand Crocs.

Real OR rubbish?

Could you crack the code?

GCHQ, the **UK intelligence agency,** decided to **recruit** spies by setting treasure hunts around the UK, and budding agents were challenged to find clues to spell out a message. Officials said anyone smart enough to solve the puzzle could become a spy.

*****Rubbish!** They didn't set treasure hunts, but GCHQ did post a puzzle on social-media platform LinkedIn. It's the first UK intelligence agency to advertise for spies on that site.

A LOT TO LEARN

Some tests may raise stress levels, but these extraordinary exam stories are more likely to raise eyebrows.

Exam stopped 90 seconds too soon

A group of 39 students in Seoul, South Korea, took legal action against the government after an exam error.

The important exam they were taking, the Suneung, usually lasts eight hours and affects university places and job options. After part of one exam (South Korea's university entrance test) finished 90 seconds early, the students wanted £12,000 each. They said this was to cover the cost of studying to retake it.

A student who really loves exams

For most students, three or four **A levels** are plenty – but Mahnoor Cheema decided to take 28.

The 17-year-old from Slough, UK, did four of these A level exams at school and the rest at home with her study partner, her mum. She had already completed 34 GCSE exams.

Cheema's extra A levels include two maths courses, three languages and three kinds of history. Her method is to "take one subject at a time", and keep up with piano, chess, swimming and seeing friends.

Real OR rubbish?

Exam gives students answer

The first question in an economics exam at Bath University, UK, gave the answer alongside the question.

The 400 students wondered whether this was a trick by the examiners, and sat through the whole paper. Once the university realised the mistake, staff apologised and said the first question would simply be ignored.

Is this story real, or have we failed the test?*

***Rubbish!** It wasn't just one question – students were accidentally given all the answers, and no one said anything. Once university staff realised, they made the students take another exam

WHAT A WAY TO LIVE!

These brave home-builders made some unusual choices.

Hop on board this family home

A couple has turned a double-decker bus into a family home. Conrad Kirk and Nicole McCarthy bought a 1978 bus that they originally used for holidays – but then they **renovated** it and moved in full-time with their four daughters.

The family created bedrooms upstairs, lots of hidden storage and a cosy reading area. They reported they saved money and could enjoy more time together.

"I feel healthier, my kids are happier and I am not as stressed as I used to be," said Kirk.

A magical indoor world preserved

Ron Gittins's flat may look ordinary on the outside, but inside is a world of colour and creativity.

Inspired by ancient Egypt and ancient Greece, Gittins spent 33 years filling the flat with his own art. There are wall paintings from floor to ceiling, handmade costumes and fireplaces shaped like mythical creatures.

The flat has now been granted Grade II listed status, meaning it is "of special interest" and should be protected.

Some of Gittins's work was based on ancient Greek and Egyptian designs.

3D-printed home

A large-scale 3D-printer robot constructed an earthquake-proof house in Guatemala.

It took 26 hours for the "printer" to squeeze out the concrete material for the 50-square-metre house's walls. Workers then installed windows, plumbing, electrical wires and a roof.

The material is **flexible**, which helps it not to break during earthquakes. This method also produces much less waste than standard building methods.

The walls are made of 'printed' concrete

FUNNY FESTIVALS

Many festivals celebrate cultural, religious and historical events. Some of them are inspired by more unusual things. Which of these do you think looks most fun?

Painting the town pink

At the start of the summer each year, the city of Vilnius, Lithuania, is painted pink for "Pink Soup Fest" in honour of the country's favourite summer dish: a kind of beetroot soup.

Thousands gather to enjoy activities such as a 50-metre-long pink slide and a huge inflatable bowl of pink soup to jump into. People dress in pink costumes, break pink-soup records and cool down with pink-soup ice cream.

Dovile Aleksandraviciene, from the city's tourism organisation, said, "It really warms the heart… with pink soup, of course."

Here comes the Sun

The sunrise festival in Inuvik, Canada, takes place each January to celebrate the Sun rising.

The natural tilt of Earth means that places such as Inuvik spend long periods either facing away from or towards the Sun – so, in mid-winter, the Sun doesn't rise for 30 days.

The festival incorporates ice skating, fireworks and music.

Celebrating citrus

During February in Menton, France, the annual Lemon Festival is held. The two-week event, which was first held in 1934, sees Menton's streets filled with sculptures and **floats** decorated with lemons and oranges.

After the event, any fruit that's still in good condition is collected. Instead of being wasted, it's sold to those who flocked to the fruity festivities.

FESTIVAL FAVOURITES

Scarecrow festival takes over a town

Every year, people in the Lancashire village of Wray, UK, make scarecrows and put them on show to raise money for charity.

Thirty-two years ago, resident David Hartnup was on holiday in France and thought he saw someone dangling from a tree. It turned out to be a scarecrow that was part of a festival, so Hartnup brought the idea back to Wray.

People go to great lengths to make their scarecrows. One family ate yoghurts for a fortnight so they could use the pots to make a Dalek.

A very cool return

During China's famous Harbin Ice Festival, a site about the size of 80 football pitches is filled with magnificent sculptures carved out of ice.

Some doubted whether the festival would return after the Covid-19 **pandemic**, as officials chose not to hold it during winter 2022–23. However, 2023–24 saw it return and draw a record 30,000 visitors every day.

Flower festivals

Flower festivals are held all around the world. There's a tulip festival in the Netherlands, a rose festival in the US and a cherry-blossom festival in Japan. A "flower carpet" is created in Belgium, and Spain holds a "flower battle"!

Blossoms become beams of light

During the Loy Krathong festival in Bangkok, Thailand, people send small baskets loaded with flowers, called "krathongs", floating down waterways. However, these often end up causing blockages.

In 2023, a new tradition was formed: to reduce waste, Thai children drew, rather than made, thousands of krathongs. These were then projected onto the water instead.

Instead of celebrating flower festivals by sending krathongs downriver, you could craft some to catch the light.

What you need

- A4 coloured card
- scissors
- a pencil
- a ruler
- glue
- coloured tissue paper
- sticky tape

1. Cut two A4 pieces of card into squares with side lengths of 21 centimetres. Fold both pieces in half, and then in half again, into quarters. Use two colours if you can.

2. Draw matching curves on the top of your folded cards, exactly as shown in the picture. Cut them out.

3. Draw a smaller curve in the middle of the folded pieces, leaving a border of 1.5 centimetres all the way around. Then cut both pieces into frames.

4. Unfold the frames and then carefully bend each crease in the opposite direction so you flatten out the card.

5. Overlap the frames with the eight points evenly spaced, and glue them together. Cut a circle frame (11 centimetres across) and stick it in the middle.

6. Cut up pieces of tissue paper and lightly glue them around the krathong – it's ok if they overlap. Turn it over to see your finished design.

Fix your finished krathong to a window with tape.

SPECTACULAR

SPORTS

TRICKY TIME-KEEPING

Sports rely on perfect timing – but sometimes it all goes wrong.

Arsenal trips up with wrong socks

A Women's Super League match between Arsenal and Chelsea was delayed by 30 minutes after Arsenal players' socks were sent off.

No one realised there was a problem until very late, when officials spotted the teams' socks were the same colour – which can be confusing on camera. Arsenal quickly had to buy black ones in the Chelsea club shop, and cover the Chelsea logo with tape.

Arsenal player Leah Williamson in the taped-up socks.

Team refuses extra play time

Two Irish basketball teams fell out when they were ordered to replay just 0.3 seconds of a match.

Portlaoise Panthers lost to Limerick Sport Eagles after two **free throws** awarded right at the end. However, Portlaoise argued the game had already finished.

After official discussions, the teams were ordered to replay 0.3 seconds of the match. Portlaoise wanted the whole game replayed, and refused.

Unfortunately, their refusal handed Limerick the win.

Students remember pigeon prank

When an annual American football game is played between US universities Harvard and Yale, one traditional tale often takes flight.

Every day during a summer vacation before one of these games, a student went down to the field in a referee shirt. They blew a referee's whistle and scattered seed, attracting flocks of pigeons.

When the day of the game came, the prank preparation paid off: pigeons descended the moment the referee first whistled. The baffled birds caused chaos, delaying the game for more than an hour.

STRETCHING
IT OUT

A bit of a stretch is always good for sports players, but these competitive contortionists take things to extremes.

Bendy teenager rolls for records

Sofia Tepla, a 14-year-old contortionist from Ukraine, earned a second Guinness World Record for her incredible ability to twist herself into seemingly impossible positions.

Tepla achieved the award for the most contortion roll push-ups in 30 seconds. She lifted her upper body 21 times while her feet hovered over her shoulders and either side of her ears.

Don't try this at home!

Contortionists bend over backwards for a good performance.

A fantastically flexible family

Amarried pair of contortionists were proud to have passed on their super-flexible skills to their children.

The couple said, "Because us parents are both able to bend, our children have both been flexible from birth. They've both grown up around contortions and it's a lot easier to learn when you start young."

The family, who originally came from Mongolia but moved to Boston, US, practised their contortionist skills together. The couple said they hoped to arrange a family show in the future.

Contortionist teen's creepy routine

Contortionist Arshiya Sharma shocked and impressed audiences with her performances on US TV talent show show *America's Got Talent*.

13-year-old Arshiya performed astonishing horror-film-themed routines that included special make-up, creepy soundtracks and well-timed sound effects that sounded like bones breaking.

After having left her home country of India for the first time to compete on the programme, the contortionist received a standing ovation and made it all the way to the quarter-finals.

ANIMAL ATHLETES

Some activities are designed for animals alone.

The world's slowest race

Each summer, the world's fastest-moving snails slide along to Norfolk, UK, to compete in the annual Snail Racing World Championships.

"Ready, steady, slow!" cries the Snail Master – and the slippery sports stars race from the centre of a circular 33 centimetre course to the finish line at the edge. The speediest snail wins a "very juicy bunch of Romaine lettuce".

The Guinness World Record was set by a snail called Archie in 1995, who completed the course in exactly two minutes.

Stingrays flaunt their soccer skills

As a football world championship was being played by humans, an underwater football game took place at the Sea Life London Aquarium. Six stingrays showed off their moves by playing with a ball full of fish.

Using teamwork and their sense of smell, the rays passed the ball around, making the fish fall out so they could be gobbled up.

Staff said the game was "a fun and **stimulating** way for the rays to eat".

Doggy paddle at Saltdean Lido

Some activities are designed for animals alone. "Dogtember" at Saltdean Lido in Brighton, UK, is a special time for water-loving dogs. It's an annual event in September that aims to raise money for the lido to keep it in good condition.

Dogs of all shapes and sizes are welcome at the sessions, and organisers estimate that more than 8,000 dogs of all breeds, with their humans, take part each year.

Lido official Deryck Chester said the month's events are "complete doggy mayhem".

MARVELLOUS MARATHONS

FACT FOCUS — What is a marathon?

A marathon is a running race that covers
42.195 kilometres.
Some marathons are for professional athletes, but thousands
of ordinary people take part in big events like the London
Marathon. These take over city streets, with many people
running for charity – some even wearing huge costumes.

A fridge too far for police officers

When police spotted someone running with a fridge strapped to their back, they believed he was a burglar and stopped him.

However, Daniel Fairbrother had a good excuse: he was training for the London Marathon. He planned to raise money for charity by completing the race carrying the hefty machine (which he called Tallulah) on his back.

Real **OR** rubbish?

Giving runners an extra kick

Sportswear company Adidas introduced a shoe with a built-in timer that caused it to split apart after 3 hours and 30 minutes, an ambitious marathon time. Athletes said the ticking timer and the fear of having to finish the race barefoot helped them stay at top speed.

Is this story real, or have we run away with the truth?*

*Rubbish! The "Pro Evo 1" wasn't built with a timer. However, it was Adidas's lightest shoe ever and was designed to last for only one race before the super-light materials wore out.

GIVE IT A GO: TUG-OF-WAR

One of the simplest but most fun sports to try is tug-of-war.

All you need to try tug-of-war is a long rope, two even teams of people and enough space to contest a match. The aim is to pull the centre point of the rope four metres from the centre line.

- To set up your game, mark a centre point on your rope and a red centre line on the ground. Mark two white lines on the ground that are each four metres away from the centre line, opposite each other.

- Set the centre point of the rope on the centre line, and have each team stand one in front of the other behind a white line, so the teams are facing each other.

- When a referee shouts "Pick up!", each team should pick up their end of the rope and get a good grip.

- When a referee shouts "Pull!", the teams should try to pull the rope's centre point over their white line.

- When a team wins two pulls, they win that match.

Tug-of-war was contested at the Olympics between 1900 and 1920.

A LONG PULL

The sport of pulling a rope is thought to go back thousands of years in different parts of the world.

HOW TO... CRAFT A SPORTY SCULPTURE

These sporty works of abstract art are based on the style of Alexander Calder.

What you need

- a sheet of thick card
- a pencil
- scissors
- paint
- paintbrushes
- a sheet of white paper
- a needle and thread

About Alexander Calder

Alexander Calder, an American sculptor and artist, was best known for inventing the moving sculpture.

1. On the sheet of card, use your pencil to draw your first abstract shape: one that looks like two figures playing sport linked together. Cut this out.

2. Draw two more shapes that look like separate figures playing the same sport. Make sure they are the same height as your original figures. Cut these out as well.

3. Cut slots in the tops or bottoms of the pieces, as shown in the picture.

4. Choose two colours. Paint your larger shape in one of them, and the other two in the other colour.

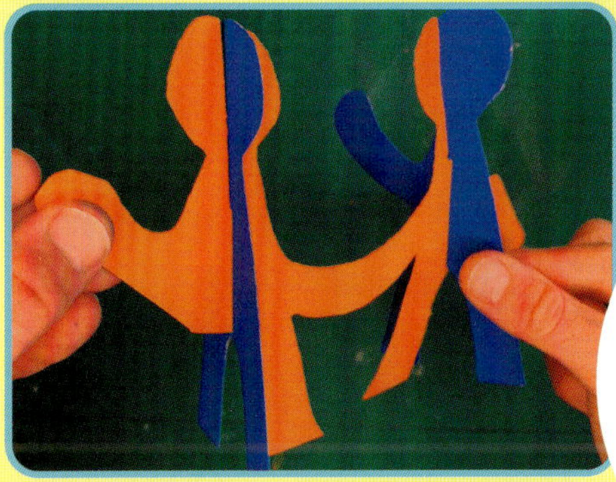

5. When they have dried completely, slot the pieces together.

6. If your stabile represents a ball sport, cut a circle of white paper and use a needle to push some thread through it (ask an adult to help you). Hang the ball between your figures – and your sporty sculpture is done!

WONDERFUL WELLBEING

MINDFUL MOMENTS
Health professionals say that paying more attention to the present moment – to our own thoughts and feelings, and to the world around us – can improve our mental wellbeing.

SPRINGING INTO SPRING

After months of winter, it lifts your spirits to see the natural world wake up in spring. You can enjoy spring the most by spending lots of time outside.

Look around

There are signs of spring all around if you look out for them.

You may spot buds growing. You might notice bees, butterflies or perhaps lambs in a field. Even in cities, you can hear birdsong and see plants growing in pavement cracks. Spring rain showers can also bring rainbows to the sky.

Look up

Mindfulness teacher Frances Trussell says it's important to look at things in different ways.

"Looking up is an important thing you can do to help keep **perspective** – when you're next outside, look up and see if you can spot something that makes you feel uplifted."

Use all your senses

You have several senses you can explore – sight, hearing, smell, taste and touch. Can you feel the breeze or sun on your skin? Can you hear birds tweeting? Can you smell new blossom?

FUN FACT
Tuning into the seasons is a great way to develop mindfulness and boost your wellbeing all year round.

Take mental snapshots

Taking photos of what you see can be a distraction as you focus on taking the picture, so try taking a mental snapshot instead.

Talk about it

Saying out loud what you're noticing can also help to keep your attention on the present moment. If you're with your family or a friend, talking about what you're spotting will help you bond over your time outdoors.

HOW TO... BRING SPRING INDOORS

It's never a good idea to disturb nature, so try simple spring-time crafts to bring a sense of the season inside.

What you need

- thick **corrugated** card (like card from a packing box)
- a ruler
- a pencil
- scissors
- paints
- a thick needle
- string or wool
- glue

1. Cut some strips from the card that are 2 centimetres wide, with the corrugated holes visible along the long edges. Cut different lengths: 16, 14, 12, 10, 8, 6 and 4 centimetres, with two strips for each of length.

2. Choose colours that remind you of springtime nature. Paint all the strips on one side, leave them to dry and then paint the other side.

3. Lightly mark the middle of each strip in pencil. Cut a piece of string or wool 80–100 centimetres long and make a knot at the end. Thread it through the middle corrugated hole in each cardboard strip. Leave the strips slightly spaced apart.

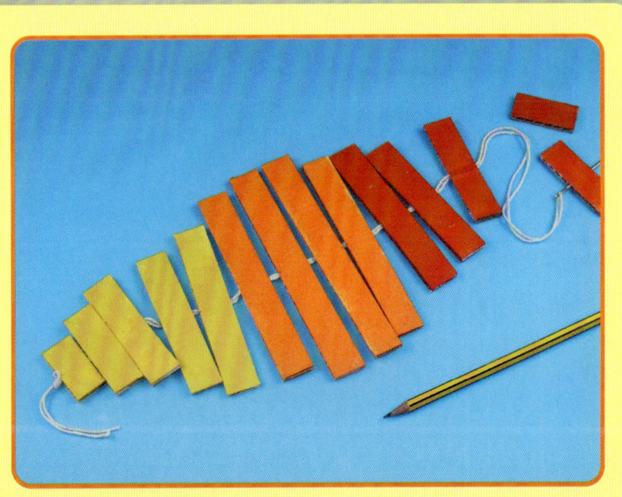

4. Dab blobs of glue in the holes around the thread and push the strips together to stick them in place. Before the glue totally dries, turn each strip at an angle to make a twisty or curvy shape.

5. Hang your spinner in the breeze and invite spring inside!

SLOWING DOWN FOR SUMMER

The long summer holidays are a great opportunity to slow down.

Compare fast and slow

During term time, most people are in a rush trying to do too much at once. This has its own name: "hurry sickness".

Compare that with life in the holidays. When you don't rush, you can enjoy your meals more, for example. When you're calm, it's easier to pack a swimming bag or picnic without forgetting anything.

How is slowing down good for you?

- Speeding through a task means cutting corners and making mistakes.

- Pausing before we act gives our brains time to find creative solutions.

- "Slowing down helps us see more," says author Amy Arthur. "There's so much we miss when we rush."

- It even helps us be better friends. A study shows we have more empathy when we take time to notice how other people feel.

A different pace

It's not always easy to stop rushing about, especially when you have lots to do. If this happens, look at tasks one by one and give yourself as much time as possible for each.

Taking quiet breaks between jobs also helps you move at a different pace. This is when summer is extra helpful: it's the perfect season to spend alone-time in the fresh air and sunshine.

GO BEACHCOMBING

If you find yourself at the beach during summer, take time to explore its environment.

What is beachcombing?

Beachcombing involves searching the seashore for interesting objects, both natural and made by humans. Common finds include sun-bleached driftwood or worn-down pebbles of glass.

You could also see chalky cuttlefish bones, round sea-urchin shells or even mermaid's purses.

Be prepared

Ask an adult to check the **tides**. It's best to go beachcombing two to three hours before or after low tide, when the beach is exposed. Dress in warm, comfortable clothes and wear wellies. Take a notebook and a camera.

Reduce your impact

Although you could pick up objects to look at them, never take away natural materials – even sand. Many objects found on beaches, like shells, are part of plants' and creatures' habitats. If you see something interesting, leave it where it was.

Get searching

Walk slowly so you can spy things. Follow the line where the tide has dropped most seaweed. Some beaches have **rock pools**, which can be mini habitats for creatures like crabs or starfish.

Look at things closely. Those tiny grey bumps on rocks are usually acorn barnacles: tiny crustaceans related to lobsters.

SLOW IT DOWN

Taking time over a sketch may help you to feel and remember the moment better than snapping a photo.

Record and learn

Take pictures, sketch or note down what you see. You might want to find out more about some discoveries later.

SNUGGLE
SEASON

Autumn is the perfect time to get warm, cosy and calm by snuggling up to recharge.

What is snuggle season?

When it's colder and darker outside, and you feel like getting cosy at home, snuggle season has arrived. It's a time for pulling on comfy clothes, enjoying warm drinks and spending time with others.

Author Meik Wiking says it's about "feeling that we're safe, and are allowing ourselves to let our guard down".

What are the benefits?

Getting warm and cosy brings calm and peace. It's a way of escaping the chilly world outside and helping you feel happier.

Spending time with friends and family also releases a feel-good chemical in your brain. This helps you feel safe, solve problems and get on with others. It also boosts your **immune system**, helping you stay healthy.

Tips for snuggling up

You don't have to try too hard to enjoy snuggle season. Getting cosy means making the most of what's around you: dim the lights, gather blankets and wear warm clothes.

Wiking suggests spending time with people you feel comfortable sharing your thoughts and feelings with. He also recommends enjoying warm, comforting food.

"It's about experiencing happiness in simple pleasures and knowing that everything is going to be OK," he says.

Snuggle-season activities to try

- Play a board game with friends and family.

- Make a playlist of your favourite relaxing tunes.

- With an adult, bake something delicious.

- Curl up for a film night.

HOST A COSY SLEEPOVER

Getting cosy with friends with a snuggle-season sleepover might be just the way to boost wellbeing.

Plan it out

Talk to your family to choose an ideal night. Decide on a start time, what friends should bring (like sleeping bags), and what time their families should pick them up in the morning.

Ask how many guests you're allowed to have, and then reach out to see who's available. If some can't sleep over, ask if they'd like to stay for the earlier part of the night.

Set the scene

Decide where you and your friends will curl up for the night. Think about how to create the cosiest atmosphere using lighting and decorations: perhaps you could hang paper autumn leaves, string up some fairy lights or use battery-operated candles.

Get comfy

Suggest that everyone wear their snuggliest pyjamas, and provide lots of pillows and blankets.

Choose comfort food for dinner – perhaps pasta or soup – and be sure to have warming snacks on hand. You could prepare some creamy hot chocolate, or bake ginger biscuits.

Have fun!

Consider games like charades, or come up with a list of films or TV shows people would enjoy.

You could also set some time aside to bond, giving everyone a chance to talk. Perhaps each person could express one worry and one thing that makes them feel grateful. Talk through each other's problems to offer comfort and advice.

BEAT THE WINTER
BLUES

Winter may feel like hard work, but you can learn to make the most of the season.

Why can winter darkness be difficult?

During winter, there's less daylight. This means you have less time outside to play with friends. It's often rainy, windy and cold, so being outside if you're not wrapped up properly isn't much fun.

FACT FOCUS — Feeling SAD?

A condition called "seasonal affective disorder" (SAD) is linked to a lack of sunlight. We need sunlight to make vitamin D, and not having enough can make you feel gloomy.

Some people battle SAD using special lamps designed to have the same brain-boosting effects as sunlight.

Get out when you can

Make the most of any sunshine, and do a bit of exercise. This will release feel-good chemicals in your brain and cheer you up. Wrap up in warm waterproof clothing, and get out in the fresh air every day.

Mental health coach Frances Trussell says it's also important for your wellbeing to keep spending time with friends and family.

Look forwards

The winter holidays around new year are a great time to reflect on the year to come. Making plans for the year ahead gives your brain a joyful jog and boosts feelings of hope.

REFLECT

ON YOUR YEAR

It can be fun to reflect on the good things that happened in your year: interesting things you did, fun places you went and goals you accomplished. Here are some things you could try.

Put together a review

At the end of the year, many newspapers and magazines create a "Year in Review" that rounds up their most popular stories. You could create your own version by writing down the year's key events. If you like, you could format it like news stories to share.

Create a top 10

A top-10 list is a fun way to recall your absolute best moments. If you get stuck, chat about it with family and friends: they might remind you of exciting events you'd forgotten. Consider asking them to make their own lists to compare, too.

Write yourself a letter

If you'd like to work through personal thoughts, you could write a letter to your future self.

Seal your letter in an envelope and mark it with the date you want to open it. That could be in six months, a year or even a few years.

When you open the envelope, you'll be able to see how you've changed and grown.

Make a scrapbook

Commemorate your year by letting your creativity shine through.

Glue printed photos from the past year into a notebook to remind you of some of your best moments. Add captions using colourful pens. To make the scrapbook extra special, decorate the pages with patterns, stickers and cuttings from newspapers and magazines.

STRANGE BUT TRUE

MIRROR MIRROR?
Mirrors facing each other don't keep reflecting forever. Each mirror absorbs a little bit of the light's energy, so the images fade away after a few hundred reflections.

ODD
OBJECTS

The unusual items that people leave behind can sometimes be surprising.

People leave the strangest things

The taxi service Uber released a remarkable list of random items left in its cars. These included a fart sensor, a cardboard cut-out panda, a personalised magic wand, a tray of meat pies, a robot and a live tortoise.

Lexi Levin Mitchel, a senior manager at Uber, said, "I'm always surprised by the wild and unique items reported lost each year."

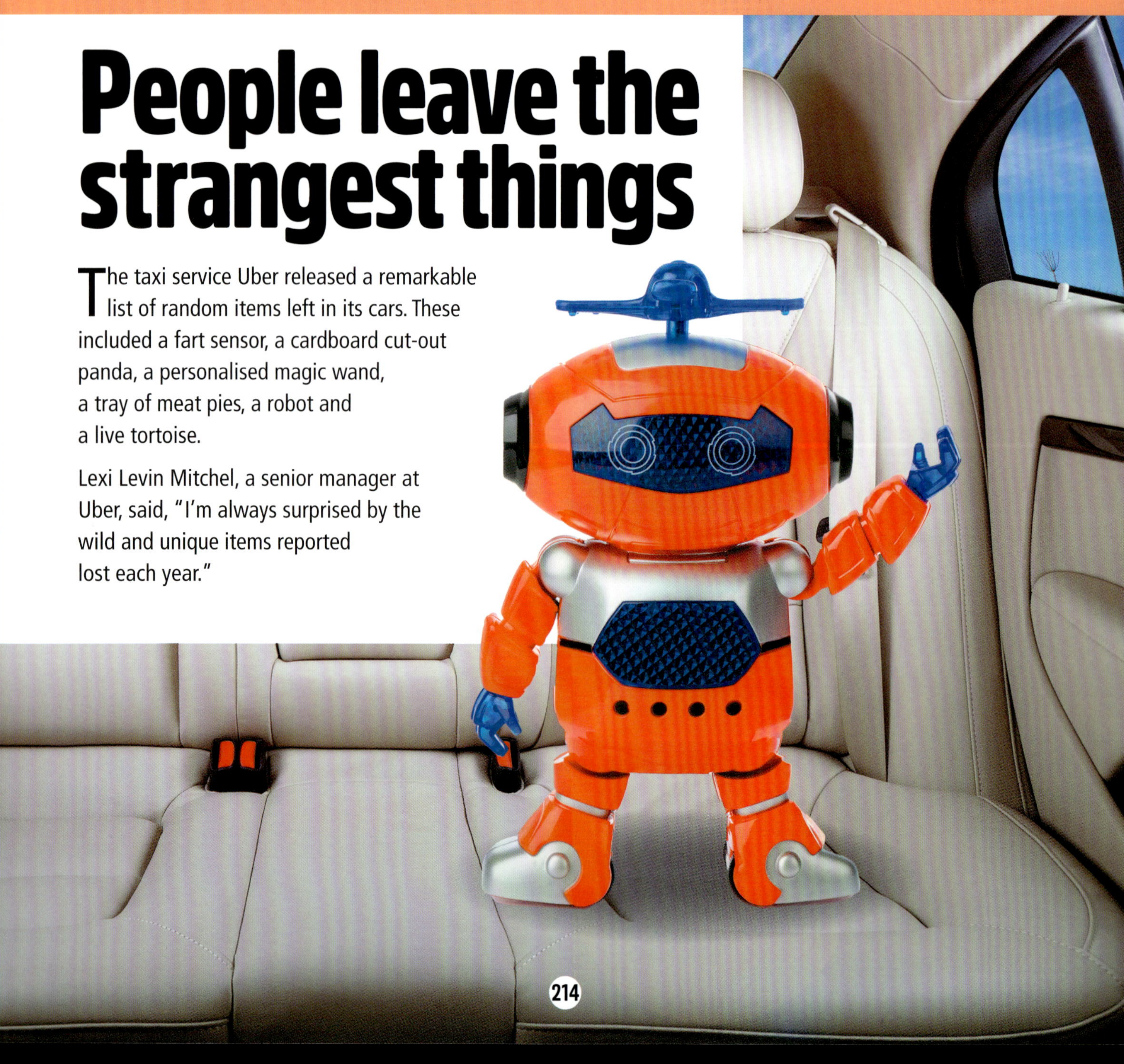

An explosive garden ornament

For years, Jeffrey and Sian Edwards enjoyed the novelty of there being what looked like a model bomb in their garden. They painted it red to match their window ledges, and Mrs Edwards often used it to remove soil from gardening tools.

However, the couple was shocked when a police officer revealed it was a real 100-year-old bomb. Experts were summoned to take it somewhere safe and blow it up immediately.

"It was an old friend," said Mr Edwards. "I'm so sorry that the poor old thing was blown to pieces."

There's no place like a gnome's home

A rock lying just off the coast of Inchcolm Island in Scotland is home to not only sea birds but also a community of gnomes.

According to one legend, the gnomes escaped from a nearby garden centre. Another suggests they were shipwrecked.

Locals report that the gnomes have been there since 2010, and mysteriously their population grows every winter. The rock is now known as "Inchgnome Island".

HAIR-RAISING!

Best beards and mega moustaches

Curly beards, twirly moustaches and many more examples of spectacular facial hair appeared at the 2023 National Beard and Moustache Championships in Florida, US.

Hundreds of people from around the country battled it out in 47 categories. The "Best in Show" winner, Jacob Darlington, received a trophy in the shape of a golden crocodile head.

Participants with beards measuring at least 20 centimetres long also united to stand in a line and connect their beards to achieve a new world record for their "beard chain", which measured 60 metres.

A reward for their hair-d work

At the world championships of **mullet** growing, only the best hairdos made the cut. Each year since 2018, thousands of people from around the world have flocked to Australia to attend Mulletfest, where enthusiasts celebrate the style and compete for prizes.

The overall winner for 2023 was Mitchell White, a 25-year-old Australian man whose father had won a prize a year earlier.

"The apple doesn't fall far from the tree," White said.

Protection for Puerto Rico's hairstyles

A law was passed to protect people's rights to hairstyles with different histories, such as afros, locs, twists and braids. The law was celebrated by campaigners because Puerto Rico's people come from lots of different backgrounds, and these hairstyles can be important parts of their **heritage**.

CRAZY FOR CARTOONS

Cartoons are loved by kids worldwide. As their popularity grows, they're also springing into life and being honoured around us.

Catbus brought to life

Electric vehicles designed to look like a famous film character have been introduced to Ghibli Park, a theme park in Japan. In the animated film *My Neighbour Totoro*, the Catbus is a living bus with 12 legs and a cat's face. The real-life Catbus has fur-covered seats and glowing eyes – but wheels instead of legs.

Dragon Ball park

A model of a Dragon Ball themed roller coaster.

The world's first theme park based on Dragon Ball and its characters is set to be opened near Saudi Arabia's capital city, Riyadh.

Dragon Ball started out as a Japanese comic in 1984 and was later turned into several television series and films. The company behind the theme park says it will have a 70-metre-tall dragon at its centre and at least 30 rides.

Driving down Charmander Lane

A new neighbourhood in Nevada, US, has named its roads after Pokémon characters.

Construction manager Andrea Miller, whose child suggested the theme for the street names, hopes that living on roads named after Squirtle and Snorlax will bring joy to residents.

If "you had a bad day," she said, "and you have to turn on Jigglypuff Lane, that will make you smile."

People often say it: if at first you don't succeed, try, try and try again!

Learner driver takes 60 tests

A learner driver finally passed their **car theory** test after 59 failed attempts. When people are learning to drive, they have to pass both a practical and a theory text to get their licence. The hour-long theory test costs £23 each time, meaning the unnamed learner spent a total of £1,380. The director of the AA driving schools took notice, complimenting the learner for their "amazing" commitment.

Friendly "failure" dog helps earthquake victims

A dog in Taiwan who failed his police training because he was too friendly and playful got a new job as part of a search-and-rescue team.

Roger, an eight-year-old Labrador retriever, became part of a team of dogs who helped to rescue people who were stranded by a big earthquake that struck Taiwan on 3 April 2024.

While he and the team saved lives, the dog's friendly face also raised spirits.

Dogs like Roger help to find and save people in trouble.

Real OR rubbish?

India puts limits on losing

A rule passed in 2024 says that people can try to get into **public office** in India only 20 times.

If a person has tried and failed to be voted in after that, officials say, they are wasting Indian voters' time and someone else should be allowed to try instead.

Cast your vote: is this real or rubbish?*

***Rubbish!** People can try as many times as they like. One man, K. Padmarajan, lost 238 elections and became known as India's "elections king". He said he was "happy losing".

WHAT'S YOUR VOTE?

Democracy may be a serious business, but some **election** efforts seem incredible.

Democracy sausages win votes

Australians have found a tasty way to bring people together on election days – by firing up their barbecues and serving sausages.

The so-called "democracy sausage" has become an election-day tradition in Australia. There are even special websites telling voters which polling stations serve the best snacks.

Peculiar places to vote

In the UK, voting can take place in all sorts of weird and wonderful places. These have included an outdoor swimming pool, a hairdresser, buses, caravans, windmills – and even someone's living room.

One strange station was opened after an emergency: when officials couldn't unlock library doors, they set up a "voting car" that was used for about an hour until the library was finally opened.

That seems unsurprising, though, compared to **NASA's** out-of-this-world option: the International Space Station has its own polling booth where astronauts can vote, listing their address as "low-Earth orbit".

Real OR rubbish?
A hopeful hippo for president

In the 2024 US election, animal-lovers could vote for Timothy, a hippo from San Antonio Zoo in Texas.

Timothy's campaign promised that, if he was elected, everyone would have legal rights to at least one nap per day and snack times in schools and offices.

Is this story real, or a hippo-sized lie?*

***Real!** The zoo launched T-shirts to promote Timothy's campaign and used the money to help protect wildlife.

PANTS
IN PUBLIC

Most people keep their underwear undercover, but these pants were put on parade.

Famous undies raise money for charity

Apair of boxer shorts sold for £330 in a charity auction. The pricey pants were part of a collection of clothing donated by singer-songwriter Ed Sheeran to a charity shop in Framlingham, UK, where Sheeran grew up.

The auction raised more than £27,000 to support **hospices** for very unwell children.

Museum in underpants record

Visitors to a museum in St Louis, US, were handed fresh underpants and asked to wear them like hats.

The unusual request was to help win a Guinness World Record for the most people wearing pants on their heads. An amazing 355 people signed up, winning the record.

The museum already owned a two-metre-wide pair of underpants. Marketing director Katy Enrique called holding the record a "natural fit" for the museum.

Real OR rubbish?
Museum's missing underwear

Underpants and stockings are just some of the thousands of objects British museums mysteriously lose every year.

The lost underwear belonged to the Victoria and Albert Museum, while Royal Museums Greenwich lost a cannonball, and more than 180 fish escaped from the Natural History Museum.

Is this story real, or have we lost track of the truth?*

*Real! More than 1,700 items – some very strange and not very valuable – are recorded as missing from British museums.

PECULIAR POOS

Astonishing toilet activity turns up everywhere!

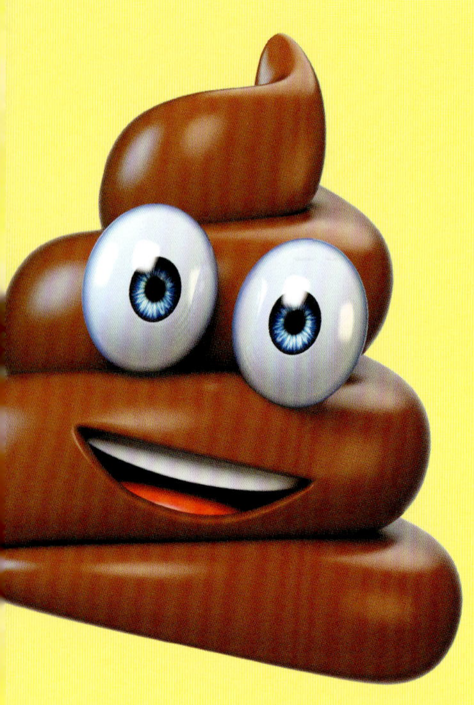

Look out for glitter poo at the zoo

At Blackpool Zoo in Lancashire, UK, zookeepers included edible glitter in food for some of their elephant residents. It's to work out whether female Asian elephants are pregnant.

Zookeepers collected the sparkling dung twice weekly and sent samples to be tested. From looking at the pretty plop, scientists could study an elephant's hormones and see if it was either pregnant or ready to start a family.

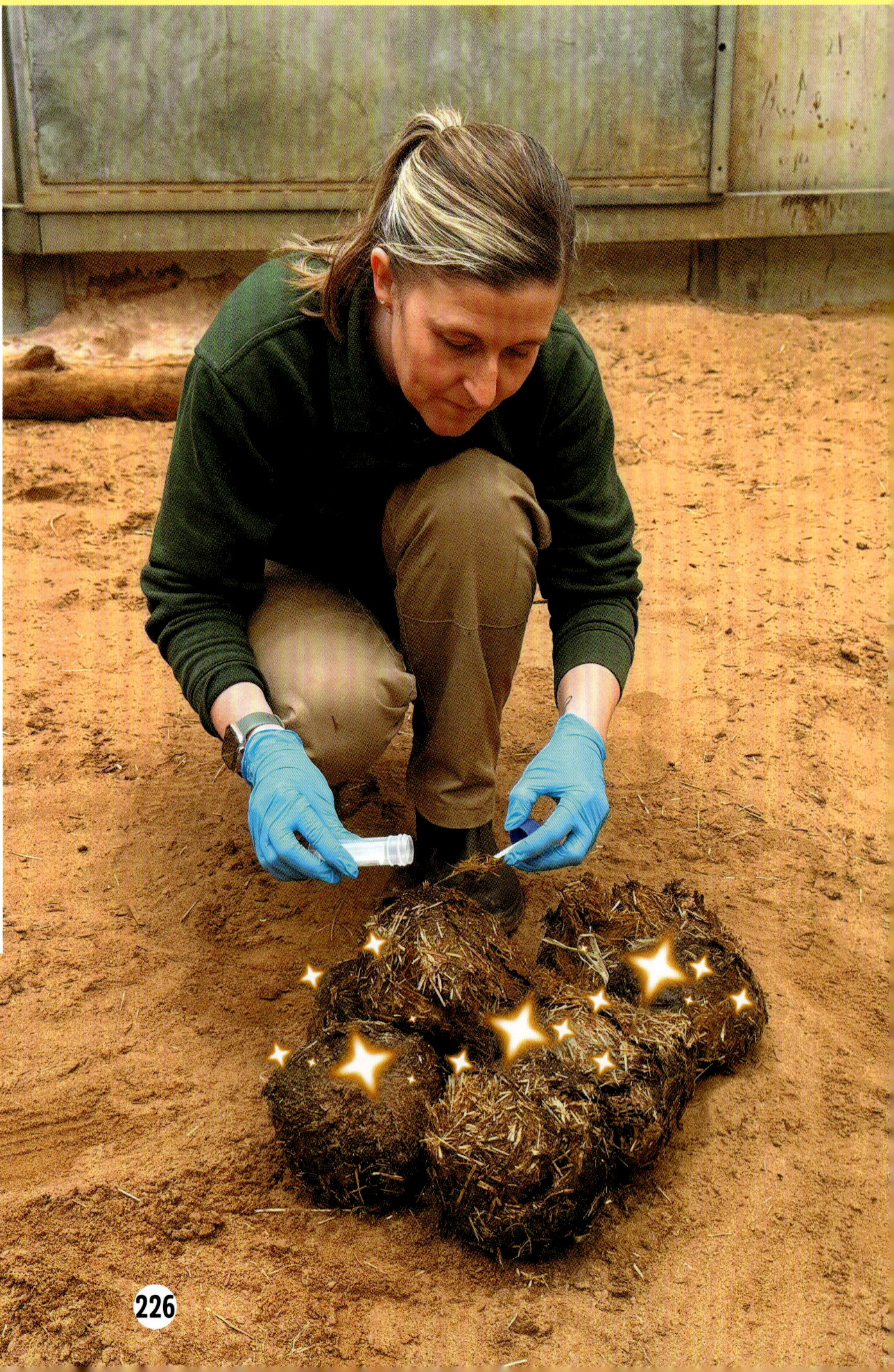

Museum's tribute to ancient poo

A man who had the world's largest coprolite collection opened a poo museum to show off his impressive hoard.

George Frandsen said he decided to set up his exhibit because there were hardly any collections of fossilised poo in other museums. The "Poozeum", in Arizona, US, became home to Frandsen's collection of more than 8,000 pieces of fossilised poo – including coprolites from dinosaurs.

Mr Frandsen saw his first coprolite as a teenager, and said he found it both funny and fascinating.

His biggest example was 67.5 centimetres long and around 70 million years old. It may have come from a Tyrannosaurus rex.

Frandsen at the Poozeum

FACT FOCUS

What is coprolite?

Coprolite is fossilised poo. It's known as a "trace fossil", meaning it's not the fossil of a living thing like an animal or plant. Trace fossils can give evidence of an animal's behaviour – in the case of coprolite, an animal's diet.

A fossilised poo

LOOPY LOOS

Ideas for lovelier loos

A competition was launched by the German Toilet Organization for people to submit ideas about how to make school toilets nicer to use.

This followed a study that found that half of German pupils avoided using school toilets because they found them so unpleasant. The winning suggestions included the addition of pot plants, disco balls, mobile-phone holders and more toilet paper.

A university teacher had to use all her brain power when she got locked in the bathroom in the ancient Cambridge University tower where she lives.

The walls of the windowless room were so thick that no one could hear Dr Krisztina Ilko calling. The cleaners weren't due until the following week, so she thought she would be stuck for days.

She used an eyeliner and a cotton bud to work on the lock, and it took seven hours – but she said it felt amazing when the door opened.

Poo rules for climbers

Mount Everest climbers now have to bring their poo back down the mountain.

Mountain climbers normally either dig a hole to be a toilet or poo out in the open. However, low temperatures meant the poo on Everest was being preserved – and so much of it had built up that it was starting to smell.

TOILET ANTICS

Golden loo thieves caught

Four men were charged with stealing a solid-gold toilet from Blenheim Palace in Oxfordshire, UK.

At the time it was taken, in 2019, the £4.8 million loo was open to the public, but there was a three-minute time limit to avoid queues. It formed part of an art exhibition, and had only been on display for two days before it was pinched. The fully-functioning 18-carat gold toilet was stolen by thieves using sledgehammers to break into the palace.

One man has already pleaded guilty to burglary, while Jones has pleaded not guilty. Two others deny the charges put to them.

The artist who created the artwork, Maurizio Cattelan, said after the theft, "Who's so stupid to steal a toilet?"

The golden toilet sculpture was called "America".

PRECIOUS PAPER

In 2013, an Australian company sold a roll of solid-gold toilet paper for $1,376,900 (a little over £1 million Australian dollars).

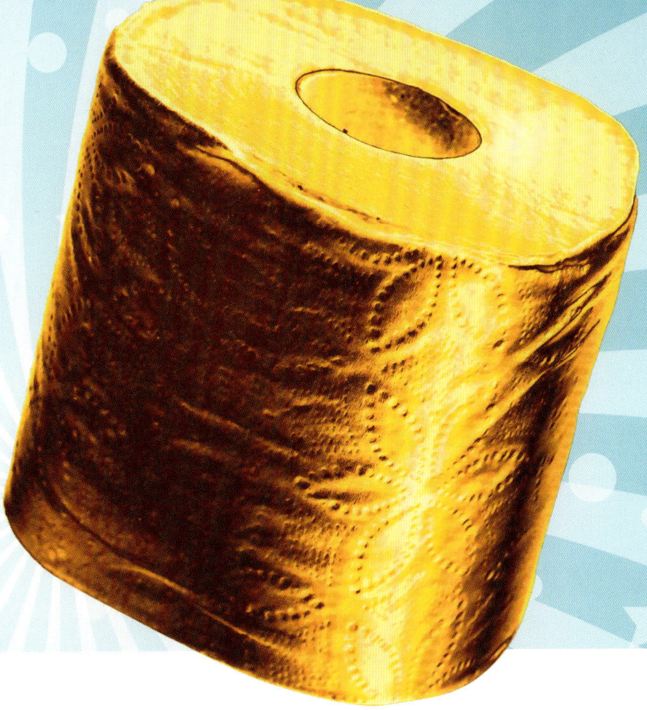

Real OR rubbish?

Ready... steady... wee!

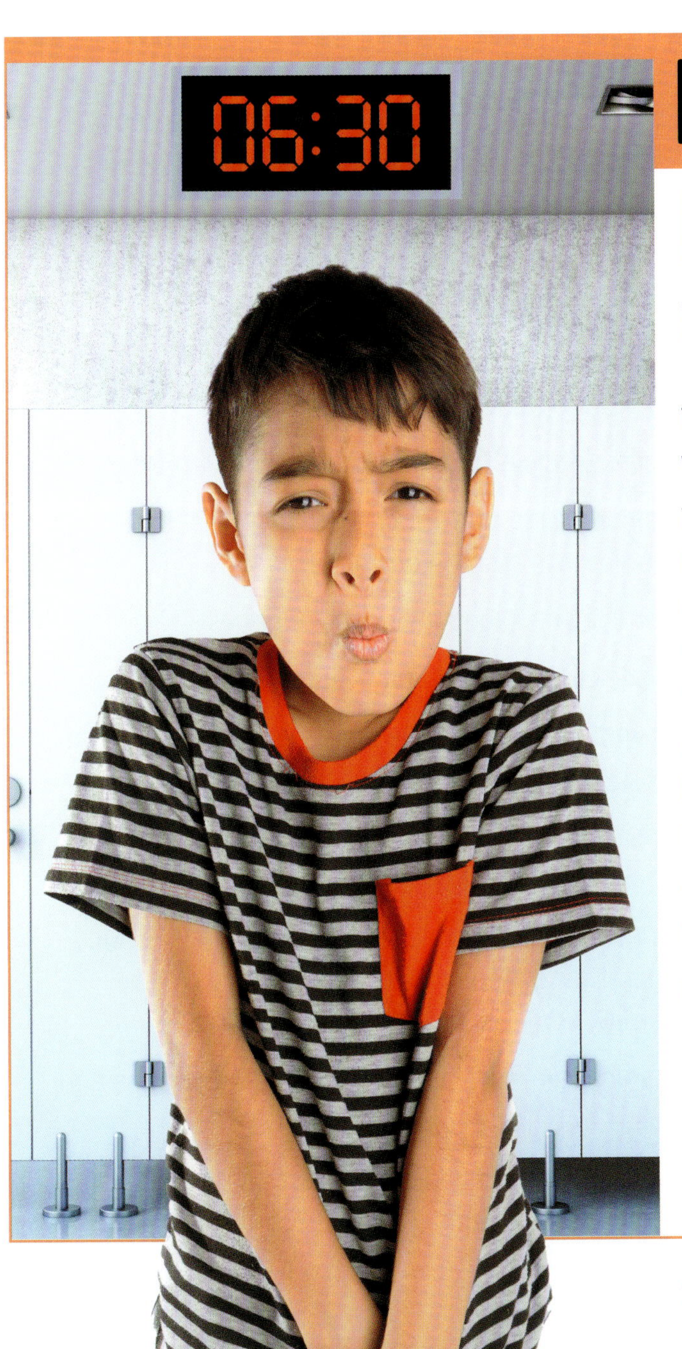

Toilets at a popular tourist site in China were fitted with timers, leaving visitors in a rush to flush.

The new system was installed at the Yungang Buddhist Grottoes, which has millions of visitors every year. While a cubicle was in use, a screen on the door showed the number of minutes and seconds the door had been locked.

A staff member said, "It's impossible that we would kick someone out midway, and we aren't setting a time limit."

One visitor found the timers "a little bit embarrassing".

Is this story real, or can you flush out a lie?*

***Rubbish!** Staff said the timers were put in to keep guests safe, in case someone became ill.

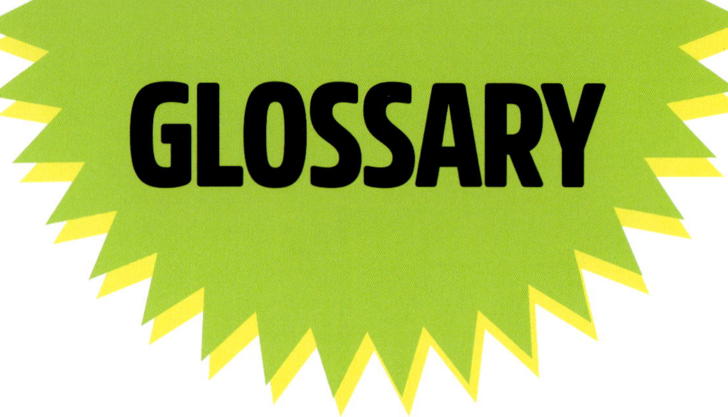

GLOSSARY

3D printers machines that create objects from digital designs by layering materials

A levels advanced-level examinations: exams taken at the end of secondary school or college, usually when people are around 18

abstract art art that doesn't show things that are recognisable but portrays them through shapes, colours and marks

accessibility how easy it is to reach or approach something

algae simple plants without stems, flowers or roots

antibiotic medicine that fights bacterial infections

anxiety a feeling of being worried and stressed

archaeologists experts who study history through ancient objects

arthritis condition that makes joints in the body stiff and painful

artificial made by humans rather than naturally occurring

auction sale where the highest bidder wins

banter jokey and playful conversation

biodiversity the variety of living things

breeding programme plan and system to help animals to reproduce

camouflaged hidden by looking like part of the surroundings

campaign planned actions to build support for change

car theory test test that quizzes learner drivers on the rules of the road

carbon chemical found in all living things, which can form carbon dioxide

carbon dioxide gas created by all living things and many human activities, which traps the Sun's heat in a layer around Earth

cargo goods carried in a vehicle

CE Common Era: after the year zero

cells tiny body parts that make up all parts of all living things

chain mail armour made from metal rings looped together

choreography planned patterns of dance steps

climate change change in average conditions, such as temperature and rainfall, over a long period of time

colony group of people or animals living together, with a shared system of organisation

concept car vehicle that has been built experimentally but not made for sale

conservation efforts to protect the environment

contortionists performers who can twist their bodies into strange positions

corrugated shaped into folds or ridges

cosseted cared for in an overindulgent way

council group of people chosen to make decisions and organise things

creativity imagination and skill, usually doing or making something unique

Crown Jewels valuable items made from precious metals and stones that are owned by a royal family

cultural related to the behaviours, knowledge and ideas that link people

curator expert in charge of what's shown in a gallery or museum

democracy type of government based on people voting for who will run the country

diagnosis the medical identification of a condition

digested absorbed into the body through the stomach

digital related to computers

DNA deoxyribonucleic acid: a chemical that carries information about how a living body is made up

Down's syndrome a brain condition that affects how people's brains and bodies develop, often linked with learning difficulties

drone remote-controlled flying robot

drought water shortage due to lack of rain

ecologists experts who study the environment

election the process of voting for people as leaders

emissions waste created by burning fuel

empathy ability to understand and share other people's feelings

eruption leak or explosion from a volcano that lets out hot melted rock

European Union group of countries in Europe that have a shared system for trading together

evolved gradually changed along the family tree, from parents to children, over an extremely long period of time

exhibition group of related displays

exhibits objects that are on display

exoskeletons hard protective skins that hold creatures' shapes without bones

expedition journey made in order to achieve something, often to explore

extinction when there is none of a species left alive

extraterrestrial from space

fjord long, deep, narrow body of seawater that reaches far inland

floats colourful wheeled platforms for parades.

forgeries items created to fool people into thinking they were made somewhere or by someone specific

fossil remains of a living thing that have been hardened into rock over an extremely long period of time

fossil fuels fuels, like coal and crude oil, that are made from decayed ancient plants and animals and are dug from the ground

free throws unblocked free shots in basketball

fungus living thing like a plant without leaves or flowers, and which doesn't use energy from the Sun (e.g. a mushroom or toadstool)

GCHQ Government Communications Headquarters: UK government agency responsible for official security and information-gathering

GCSE General Certificate of Secondary Education: exam taken at the end of Year 11/5th form, usually when people are around 16

genes parts of cells that control certain ways a body is made up (such as eye colour), passed down from parents

genre style or category (of books, films, music or art)

gills organ used by fish and other creatures to breathe underwater

glacier large area of thick ice that moves like a river but extremely slowly, usually staying frozen

gladiator fighter in ancient Roman shows that were put on for entertainment

Guinness World Record one of a collection of records of people's achievements, which were originally released annually in a book

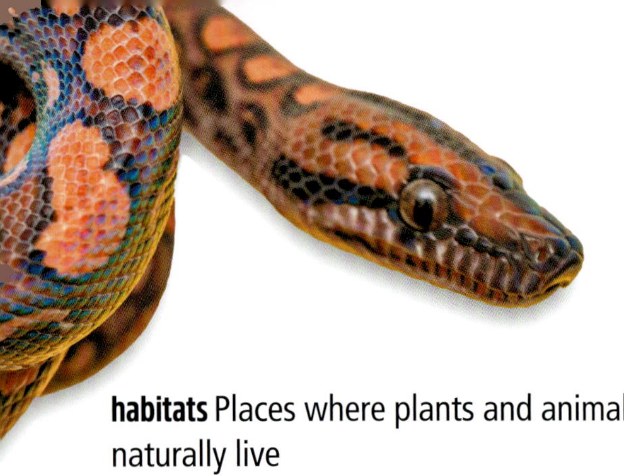

habitats Places where plants and animals naturally live

heritage special traditions and beliefs passed down through generations

hormones chemicals in the body that control developments like growth

hospices places where people can live and receive care when they are very sick

humidity amount of moisture in the air

immune system body system that fights illness

implant something that is put into the body to affect how it works or looks

indigenous originally from a particular place

innovative using new approaches to solve a problem or achieve a goal

inspired created or affected by a different experience

installation art that is made for a specific place

invasive coming in from somewhere else and taking over

landslide movement of crumbling land as it slides downhill

lido an outdoor pool or beach area

limbs body parts that stick out, such as arms, legs, wings or tails

literacy ability to read and write

livestock farm animals

maintenance keeping something in good condition

meteorite a rock or metal from space that falls to Earth

microscope device that makes tiny things look bigger

minister a government official in charge of a particular area

monitored watched and recorded

mullet hairstyle that is short on the top and sides, and longer at the back

NASA National Aeronautics and Space Administration: US government agency responsible for space research and exploration

natural disasters serious problems caused by natural processes like weather (including earthquakes, floods and violent storms)

nerves body parts that carry messages to and from the brain, for example allowing feeling and movement

nutrients chemical substances that are needed by living things, usually found in food

offal animals' internal body parts (such as hearts, lungs and stomachs) that are used by people as food

opera a play where most of the words are sung

organ a musical instrument with pipes, played with keys like a piano's

organisms individual living things like animals and plants

palaeontologists experts who study fossils

pandemic a disease that spreads quickly all over the world

Parkinson's disease a condition that damages how the brain controls movement, which gets worse over time

perspective how you see or think about something from a particular direction or with a particular set of ideas

pest-resistant able to survive attacks from insects or other pests.

plant-based made only from things that can be taken or created from plants

pollinates spreads pollen between plants, meaning their seeds are able to grow

pranksters people who play practical jokes or tricks

predators creatures that catch and eat other creatures

prosthetic an artificial body part

protests actions taken to show disagreement

psychologists experts who study how people think

public office a position of power in the government

recruit invite to join an organisation

refugee person who has had to leave their home country because of war or the threat of violence

rehome take to live somewhere new

renewable energy energy from sources that will never run out, like wind and sun

repurpose find a new use for something old

reservoir place built to store water, like a human-made lake

resources things that are useful or valuable

rock pools small pools of water left behind by the sea after the tide goes out

rodents small mammals with sharp teeth like mice, rats and squirrels

rover small remote-controlled robot that travels across land to explore it

RSPCA Royal Society for the Prevention of Cruelty to Animals: UK charity with the aim of protecting animals

sanctuary a safe place for animals or people

scarce not enough of something

sensors devices that pick up physical changes like movement or temperature

sign language language that uses hand movements to communicate used by people who are deaf or hard of hearing

single-use plastic plastic items that can only be used once, like straws and bags

social relating to how people or animals interact with each other

social media apps and websites that allow users to connect with each other online

species type of animal or plant with similar features that regularly have babies together

static electricity a type of electricity generated by movement

status your position or rank compared to others

stimulating exciting and interesting

summary brief description containing only main points

syllable part of a word, or a whole word, made up of one beat (for example, one of the three in syll-a-ble)

tentacles flexible and movable body parts used for holding things, travelling and feeding

territory an area that an animal or group claims as their own

theory an idea that tries to explain something

tides natural rises and falls of the sea every day, caused by forces from the Moon and Sun

tracking tags small devices that help track the location of animals or other things.

treadmill a machine you can walk or run on while staying in the same place.

trialling testing something to see whether it works

upcycling reusing old items to create new things

UV light a type of light you can't see, but it can make some things glow

vertebrate animal with a spine

virtual reality set of computer images creating what seems like a realistic space, which can be explored and affected by the people or other animals within it

water purifier a device that cleans water

whittle to carve wood by shaving off small pieces

INDEX

in space 110–111
  super-sized 152–153
  waste 82
  Welsh rarebit recipe 156–157
football 103, 182–183
forest fires 72
forests 69
fossil fuels 67
fossils 76–77, 227
frogs 17, 50–51
fungus 161

G

geckos 31
ghost bus 167
giant apes 77
gifts 83
glaciers 70
global warming 74–77
glowing animals 40
gnomes 215
great crested grebes 17

H

haikus 124
hair 216–217
heaviest animal 32
hippopotamuses 31, 223
holidays 160–161
homes 172–173
hope 209
horses 12, 18
hummingbirds 34–35

I

ice festival 177
iguanas 44
inclusivity 88–89
indigenous languages 87
insects 58–59, 143
inventions 102–105

J

jellyfish 33
jetpacks 90
jobs 168–169
journaling 120–123, 210–211

K

kangaroos 11
karaoke 117

L

languages 87, 107
lemurs 14
libraries 114–117
limericks 125

M

manga 219
marathon running 188–189
mental health 204–209
mice 26, 41, 67, 101
microbes 96
mindfulness 194
mirrors 213
modern art 128
mud 78

music 138–139
  animals 14–17
  nose whistling 138
  rapping 139

N

nacho recipe 154–155
NASA 108–111, 223
national parks 29, 43, 67, 164
newts 42
Niue 65

O

octopuses 54
orangutans 15, 20
ocean conservation 52–55, 78–79

P

parrotfish 53
parrots 10
penguins 27–28
pigeons 38–39, 183
pizza 148–151
plants 74–75
plastic pollution 69
platypuses 40
poetry 124–125
Pokémon 219
polar bears 29
politics 86, 222–223
pollution 69, 73
Pompeii 95
poo 226–227, 229
prosthetic limbs 104
pygmy hippopotamus 31

IMAGE CREDITS

Front cover (tl (footballer)) Alex Burstow/Contributor/Getty Images; (tr (alligator)) reptiles4all/Shutterstock; (mr (sunglasses emoji)) Igillustrator/Shutterstock; (mr (heart eyes and kiss emojis)) Zuhri Alka/Shutterstock; (mr (hummingbird)) Glass and Nature/Shutterstock; (br (astronaut)) Dima Zel/Shutterstock; (bl (shark)) Jsegalexplore/Shutterstock; (ml (gecko)) Binturong-tonoscarpe/Shutterstock; p2 (t) phive/Shutterstock; (b) Yana Lyso/Shutterstock; p3 tanazura/Shutterstock; p4 (t) stockphoto mania/Shutterstock; (b) luscofusco/Shutterstock; p5 (t (placard)) photka/Shutterstock; (t (globe)) Yaroshenko Olena/Shutterstock; (ml) HomeArt/Shutterstock; (mr) New Africa/Shutterstock; (bl) kak2s/Shutterstock; (br) MP Art/Shutterstock; p6 (t) Master1305/Shutterstock; (b) Yeti studio/Shutterstock; p7 (t) irin-k/Shutterstock; (m) Pixel-Shot/Shutterstock; (b) Tatiana Popova/Shutterstock; p8–9 Miroslav Srb/Shutterstock; p10 (t) Yana Lyso/Shutterstock; (b) Eric Isselee/Shutterstock; p11 (t) LifetimeStock/Shutterstock; (m) Steve Travelguide/Shutterstock; (b (budgie)) xpixel/Shutterstock; (b (space suit)) Rick Partington/Shutterstock; p12 (bg) Evina Milenova/Shutterstock; (b) Rita_Kochmarjova/Shutterstock; p13 Tomas Hulik ARTpoint/Shutterstock; (b) Nancy Pauwels/Shutterstock; p14 (t) Martial Red/Shutterstock; (b) Jordi Jornet/Shutterstock; p15 (t) Yusnizam Yusof/Shutterstock; (b) Olga Gauri/Shutterstock; p16 (l) photomaster/Shutterstock; (r) Anake Seenadee/Shutterstock; p17 (t) Frank Cornelissen/Shutterstock; (b) dim.vil/Shutterstock; p18 (bg) trucic/Shutterstock; (t) Ermolaev Alexander/Shutterstock; (b) AnnGaysorn/Shutterstock; p19 (t) Altrendo Images/Shutterstock; (b) © April Kline 2025, used with permission; p20 (t) PRANEE JIRAKITDACHAKUN/Shutterstock; (m) AFP PHOTO/SUAQ Foundation/Getty Images; (b) AFP PHOTO/SUAQ Foundation/Getty Images; p21 (t) Jo-anne Hounsom/Shutterstock; (m) Patrick Rolands/Shutterstock; (b) Johannes Kornelius/Shutterstock; p22 (t) YK/Shutterstock; (b) nuu_jeed/Shutterstock; p23 (bg) Hananeko_Studio/Shutterstock; (t) GoodFocused/Shutterstock; (b) Anom Harya/Shutterstock; p24 (t) Zeroeight.Studio/Shutterstock; (m) SWNS; (b) annokhotska/Shutterstock; p25 (t (palace)) Kamira/Shutterstock; (t (cat)) Iryna Kuznetsova/Shutterstock; (t (hands)) New Africa/Shutterstock; (t (cat food)) Hekla/Shutterstock; (b) Sylvie Pabion Martin/Shutterstock; p26 © Jeff De Boer 2025, used with permission; p27 (t (towel)) Roman Samborskyi/Shutterstock; (t (cow)) Clara Bastian/Shutterstock; (b) UPI/Alamy Live News; p28 (bg) karenfoleyphotography/Shutterstock; (b) Mogens Trolle/Shutterstock; p29 (t) Russell Millner/Alamy; (b) Anne Vlietstra/Shutterstock; p30 Imagefoto55/Shutterstock; p31 (t) Picture by Tambako the Jaguar/Getty Images; (bl) reptiles4all/Shutterstock; (br) John Carnemolla/Shutterstock; p32 dpa picture alliance/Alamy Stock Photo; p33 (t) d3_plus/Shutterstock; (m) Darla Zelenitsky, University of Calgary (specimen courtesy of Royal Tyrrell Museum), used with permission; (b) luscofusco/Shutterstock; p34–35 Ondrej Prosicky/Shutterstock; p36 (bg) ER_09/Shutterstock; (b) Mike Truchon/Shutterstock; p37 (t (kestrel)) WildMedia/Shutterstock; (t (art supplies)) New Africa/Shutterstock; (t (beret)) Dani Simmonds/Shutterstock; (b (car)) Rawpixel.com/Shutterstock; (b (road)) anggakrnwaan/Shutterstock; (b (person)) Cookie Studio/Shutterstock; (b (hen)) stockphoto mania/Shutterstock; p38–39 (t) drpnncpptak/Shutterstock; p38 (m) Sriram Bird Photographer/Shutterstock; (b) Christopher PB/Shutterstock; p39 (b) a2driano/Shutterstock; p40 (t) WildLens Photograph/Shutterstock; (b) M Harits Fadhli/Shutterstock; p41 (t (mouse)) Eric Isselee/Shutterstock; (t (broom)) Artiom Photo/Shutterstock; (b) Milan Zygmunt/Shutterstock; p42–43 (bg) JaklZdenek/Shutterstock; p42 (t) Florian Bott/Shutterstock; p44 tok anas/Shutterstock; p45 (t) Baishev/Shutterstock; (m) IrinaK/Shutterstock; (b (police officer)) SWNS; (b (flooded road)) PJ photography/Shutterstock; p46–47 (bg) ShutterOK/Shutterstock; p46 (b) Hans Denis Schneider/Shutterstock; p47 (t) Murilo Mazzo/Shutterstock; p48 axolotlowner/Shutterstock; p49 (t) © Renato Gaiga 2025, used with permission; (b) JacobLoyacano/Shutterstock; p50–51 (bg) Minden Pictures/Alamy Stock Photo; p50 (b) Dirk Ercken/Shutterstock; p51 (t) © Abhijit Das 2025, used with permission; p52 (bg) Rich Carey/Shutterstock; (m (fish)) Pavaphon Supanantananont/Shutterstock; (m (sound effects)) Fourleaflover/Shutterstock; p53 (t) Marion Kraschl/Shutterstock; (m) aquapix/Shutterstock; (bl) Vac1/Shutterstock; (br) Vac2/Shutterstock; p54–55 (bg) Blanscape/Shutterstock; p55 (t) Svitlana Kasianenko/Shutterstock; (m) Kletr/Shutterstock; (b) belizar/Shutterstock; p56–57 (bg) I Wayan Sumatika/Shutterstock; p56 (b (spider crab)) PRILL/Shutterstock; (b (mussels)) innakreativ/Shutterstock; p57 (m (crab)) duangnapa_b/Shutterstock; (m (score paddle)) New Africa/Shutterstock; (m (laughing emojis)) nazgraph1cs/Shutterstock; p58 (t) unpict/Shutterstock; (b) Imabulary/Shutterstock; p59 (t) Ttstudio/Shutterstock; (m) Andreas Vogel/Shutterstock; (bl) panor156/Shutterstock; (bm) irin-k/Shutterstock; (br) irin-k/Shutterstock; p60 Henrik Larsson/Shutterstock; p61 (tl) The Natural History Museum/Alamy Stock Photo; (tr) Aldiiprstio/Shutterstock; (b) CandyRetriever/Shutterstock; p62–63 (bg) Tanja Vera/Shutterstock; p62 (tl) volschenkh/iStock by Getty Images; (tr) Berto Ordieres/Shutterstock; p63 (t) © London Zoo, used with permission; p64–65 (DPS) Matous Vins/Shutterstock; p66 (t) HomeArt/Shutterstock; (b) Romaine W/Shutterstock; p67 (t) Neil Bowman/Shutterstock; (m) phive/Shutterstock; (b) Rezamonium/Shutterstock; p68 bombermoon/Shutterstock; p69 (t) Manhattan Healing Forest, New York City, USA, Courtesy of SUGi, used with permission; (b) photka/Shutterstock; p70 (t) JosepPerianes/Shutterstock; (b) Associated Press/Alamy Stock Photo; p71 Abdulghafur Anasi/Shutterstock; p72 NataliaCatalina.com/Shutterstock; p73 (tl) stockpexel/Shutterstock; (tr) Richard Juilliart/Shutterstock ; (b) Maria_Andreevna/Shutterstock; p74 (bg) Ellieg93/Shutterstock; (b) smthtp/Shutterstock; p75 (t) Suthin_Saenontad/Shutterstock; (m) Sam Trench/Shutterstock; (b) Ou Chantha/Shutterstock; p76 (t) OlgaBombologna/Shutterstock; (b) slonme/Shutterstock; p77 (bg) EAKARAT BUANOI/Shutterstock; (m) © Renaud Garcia/Joannes–Boyau 2024, used with permission; p78 (t) Debra Angel/Shutterstock; (b) Aestels/Shutterstock; p79 (bg) GizemG/Shutterstock; (b) Domingo Saez/Shutterstock; p80–81 (bg) mspoli/Shutterstock; p80 (b) Vladimir Sukhachev/Shutterstock; p81 (l) GRACIELLADEMONNE/Shutterstock; (r) Amada Ekeli/Shutterstock; p82 Joe Belanger/Shutterstock; p83 (t) Roman Samborskyi/Shutterstock; (ml (cinema audience)) Summit Art Creations/Shutterstock; (ml (restaurant)) Dragon Images/Shutterstock; (bl (science exhibit)) Monkey Business Images/Shutterstock; (br (museum)) David Tadevosian/Shutterstock; (b (photos and tape)) zmshv/Shutterstock; p84–85 Holli/Shutterstock; p86 JOSE JORDAN/Contributor/Getty Images; p87 (tl) Steve Russell/Contributor/Getty Images; (tr) wavebreakmedia/Shutterstock; (b) Timur Malazoniia/Shutterstock; p88 (t) Eamonn M. McCormack/Stringer/Getty Images; (bl (girl tapdancing)) adamkaz/iStock by Getty Images; (bm (boy in jeans)) Kelli Seeger Kim/Stocksy; (bm (boy doing ballet)) Sean Nel/Shutterstock; (br (wheelchair user)) SolStock/iStock by Getty Images; p89 (t) MADS CLAUS RASMUSSEN/Contributor/Getty Images; (m) wavebreakmedia/Shutterstock; (b) Paolo Gallo/Shutterstock; p90 Anadolu/Contributor/Getty Images; p91 (bg) © Loen Active/Kjersti Kvamme 2024, used with permission; (b) Associated Press/Alamy Stock Photo; p92 Daily Herald Archive/Contributor/Getty Images; p93 (t) Marzolino/Shutterstock; (b) Heritage Images/Contributor/Getty Images; p94 acsen/Shutterstock; p95 (t) Nataliya Schmidt/Shutterstock; (m) DEA/G. NIMATALLAH/Contributor/Getty Images; (b) Goskova Tatiana/Shutterstock; p96–97 Inside Creative House/Shutterstock; p98 (bg) Roman Zaiets/Shutterstock; (m) BSIP SA/Alamy Stock Photo; p99 (t) The Asahi Shimbun/Contributor/Getty Images; (b) Africa Studio/Shutterstock; p100 SOPA Images/Contributor/Getty Images; p101 (t) Kyodo News/Contributor/Getty Images; (b) © Zenshan Bing 2025, used with permission; p102 Evgeny Haritonov/Shutterstock; p103 (t) PA Images/Alamy Stock Photo; (m) irin-k/Shutterstock; (b) Xinhua/Alamy Stock Photo; p104 (bg) JomyenchaT/Shutterstock; (m) HENNING BAGGER/Contributor/Getty Images; p105 (t) Max4e Photo/Shutterstock; (b) GABRIEL MONNET/Contributor/Getty Images; p106–107 (bg) Studio Romantic/Shutterstock; p106 (emojis) Setia Abadi Art/Shutterstock; p107 (emoji) nazgraph1cs/Shutterstock; p108–109 (bg) alexkoral/Shutterstock; p108 NASA; p109 (t) Dima Zel/Shutterstock; (b) European Space Agency – ESA, used with permission; p110 (bg) Frame Stock Footage/Shutterstock; p111 (t) Wirestock Creators/Shutterstock; (b) Xinhua Alamy Stock Photo; p112–113 FamVeld/Shutterstock; p114 (t) New Africa/Shutterstock; (b) Simone Padovani/Awakening/ Contributor/Getty Images; p115 (bg) laksena/Alexandru Nika/Shutterstock; (m) Boston Globe/Contributor/Getty Images; p116 (t) Passakorn Umpornmaha/Shutterstock; (b) goir/Shutterstock; p117 (tl (frame)) tete_escape/Shutterstock; (tl (cat drawing)) sonkotra/Shutterstock; (tr) Walter Bibikow/Getty Images; (b) NurPhoto/Contributor/Getty Images; p118 (t) Billion Photos/Shutterstock; (b) Roman Samborskyi/Shutterstock; p119 (bg) trucic/Shutterstock; (t) Fred Duval/Shutterstock; (m) Dave Benett/Contributor/Getty Images; (b) Eddie Keogh – The FA/Contributor/Getty Images; p120 (bg) natrot/Shutterstock; (m) Svetlana Khutornaia/Shutterstock; (b) MP Art/Shutterstock; p121 (t) Olena Dumanchuk/Shutterstock; (m) Roman Samborskyi/Shutterstock; (b) Sasha Is/Shutterstock; p122 Ruslan Huzau/Shutterstock; p123 Ground Picture/Shutterstock; p124–125 (bg) natrot/Shutterstock; p124 (t) Dontrell Mompoint/Shutterstock; (bl) New Africa/Shutterstock; (br) rawf8/Shutterstock; (bl) New Africa/Shutterstock; p125 (t) New Africa/Shutterstock; (b) Pixel-Shot/Shutterstock; p126–127 Geobor/Shutterstock; p128 Roma Ashraf/Shutterstock; p129 (t) Boyloso/Shutterstock; (m) FedevPhoto/Alamy Stock Photo; (b) Alicia G. Monedero/Shutterstock; p130 GONZALEZ OSCAR/Alamy Stock Photo; p131 (t (painting)) steeve-x-art/Alamy Stock Photo; (t (frame)) LiliGraphie/Shutterstock; (b (man with picture frame)) Pixel-Shot/Shutterstock; (b (painted flower)) Africa Studio/Shutterstock; (b (picture frames)) Aliaksei Kaponia/Shutterstock; (b (eye painting)) Mari Dein/Shutterstock; (b (landscape painting)) aniroot.cdd/Shutterstock; (b (still life)) VIS Fine Art/Shutterstock; p132 (bg) Alzay/Shutterstock; (b) SWNS; p133 (tl) Charlie J Ercilla/Alamy Stock Photo;